CALLED TO KILL

CALLED TO KILL

Joan Albarella

RISING TIDE PRESS

G:FT
3-06

Rising Tide Press
3831 N. Oracle Road
Tucson, AZ 85705
520-888-1140

Printed in the United States on acid-free paper.

Publisher's note:
All characters, places, and situations in this book are
fictitious, and any resemblance to persons (living or
dead) is purely coincidental.

Cover art by MacGraphics

First Printing: April 2000
10 9 8 7 6 5 4 3 2 1

            Albarella, Joan 1944 –
            Agenda for Murder/Joan Albarella
                  p.cm

ISBN 1-883061-28-8

Library of Congress Control Number: 00-132691

DEDICATION

To Karen Whitney for her encouragement, creativity and especially her help with editing and promotion.

To my family, friends, and book club for all their support.

And to Debra and Brenda, the new owners of Rising Tide Press for their courage and commitment to women writers.

ABOUT THE AUTHOR

Joan Albarella is the author of four books of poetry and two mystery novels. She loves writing but also enjoys her work as an Associate Professor in Writing at an adult education center in Buffalo, New York.

Joan lives in the artist, Charles Burchfield's house with her companion cat, Pearl. She has a special passion for quaint small towns, Sunday pasta, spirituality, slot machines, and humor.

CHAPTER 1

Trang walks softly and slowly across the thick, spongy, vermilion rug in the lobby of the Buffalo Hyatt Regency Hotel. She stops just within touching distance of Nikki. But Nikki's full attention is on a large wall poster advertising an art exhibit by Mary York.

"I've reserved a room," Trang nervously says in a hushed voice to Nikki's back. "We can go up now."

Nikki jumps slightly and turns. Taken off guard by Trang's noiseless arrival, Nikki asks quizzically, "Reserved a room?"

They're finally face to face. The twenty-five years since their last meeting begins to melt away, like wax too close to a flame. They're no longer forty-year-old women standing in a hotel lobby in Buffalo....

They travel back in time to 1972. Trang is nineteen, and Nikki is twenty-two. They're in a cheap hotel on the lower end of Thai Hoc Street in Saigon. Nikki is drunk—overcome with grief and vengeance. Her lover, Lieutenant Maureen Mo Matthews is dead, killed when a Viet Cong bomb ripped apart the restaurant where she waited for Nikki.

Emotionally dead, Nikki carefully plots her revenge. She plans to murder a Vietnamese woman the same age as Mo. Trang, unknowingly, is the woman Nikki will kill. Trang represents all the Viet Cong enemies who hurt Nikki in this war. In reality, Trang works the streets as a prostitute in order to support her Amerasian child. The American soldiers in Vietnam pay well for prostitutes, but take no responsibility for the thousands of babies born out of their wartime recreation.....

"The room is 'no smoking'." Trang jolts Nikki back to the present, as she continues to talk in an almost whisper. "Is that okay?"

Nikki doesn't say anything, just continues to stare at Trang.

Trang finally breaks the intense eye contact by dangling the room keys in front of Nikki.

Nikki's face twitches into a nervous smile. She remembers how Trang always had the upper hand, mostly out of sheer assertiveness and persistence. "What room? You didn't say anything about a room on the phone."

Trang smiles, and Nikki observes how beautiful she still is. Her long black hair has a few strands of gray that create sparkles under the lobby chandelier. Her make-up is understated and flawless, and she wears a gray Gucci business suit, complete with mini-skirt and matching gray heels.

"I thought you wanted to talk to me about something very important." Nikki relaxes somewhat, trying to take back control.

"I do." Trang quickly drops the smile, looking serious again. "I need your help, Barnes. I thought the room would be convenient for both of us...and private. I'd rather not be seen today."

When Trang calls her "Barnes," Nikki's memory again rolls back to NAM. Her name was hand printed on all of her uniforms for identification, just like all the other soldiers. Trang became Nikki's Mama San...did her laundry and cleaning for a very small amount of money..."Barnes" was the only name Trang ever used for her.

Nikki shakes these memories from her mind and focuses back on the present situation.

Taking a step closer to Trang, she says, "Let's go to the room. I quit smoking years ago."

"I still owe you a three thousand dollar lay." Trang whispers and smiles, as Nikki crosses in front of her to lead the way to the elevators.

Nikki's face heats up in a rising blush. This was the amount of money Nikki loaned Trang, so she and her child could bribe their way out of Vietnam. Trang promised to repay the money someday, one way or another. Nikki stops and turns back. They're only inches apart now, as she says, "I thought you could afford to repay in cash now." Then lowering her voice even further, she continues, "I read in the business pages that your husband is a millionaire."

"Money isn't everything." Trang is visibly overcome with sadness.

"I never thought I'd hear you say that!" Nikki tries to lighten up the conversation, but she doesn't change Trang's sad demeanor.

"I thought once that money could do anything," Trang answers. "I was wrong."

Nikki feels the fear in Trang's voice and quickly adds, "Let's go to that room."

Trang looks straight ahead and joins Nikki's step as they move to the elevator.

✄

Room 604 is one of the Hyatt's expensive, private suites. A row of windows on the far wall greets the guests as they enter the room. The windows provide a panoramic view of the Buffalo Skyline and sparkling waterfront. A contemporary mahogany frame outlines the king-size bed, and a white quilted coverlet matches the pattern in the chair and sofa across the room from the bed. A small stocked bar is behind the sofa, and a glass topped table in front of the sofa is set with crystal plates and matching water glasses, cutlery, china cups and saucers. On a rolling cart to the side of the sofa are several platters with silver covers.

Trang enters the room first; Nikki follows. Trang goes directly to the bar. "I hope you don't mind, Barnes. I've ordered some lunch, to save time." She turns back. "Would you like a drink? I'm going to have one."

Not waiting for an answer, she pours herself a bourbon and water. Then takes a quick sip. She moves another glass close to the bourbon bottle and looks at Nikki for an answer.

"None for me." Nikki says, nervously combing her fingers through her disheveled, curly blonde hair.

Trang picks up her glass and takes a larger swallow. "Gave drinking up altogether, have you, Barnes?"

Nikki isn't comfortable being called by her military surname, but she doesn't flinch, just pats the gray streak of hair above the left side of her forehead.

"But now you're Reverend Barnes or Professor Barnes." Trang moves to the sofa with her drink and sits down. "Or perhaps you would like to be called 'Nicolette'."

"My name is Nikki." Nikki almost snaps as she moves closer to the sofa. "My name was always Nikki."

Trang takes another big swallow. "Barrett always calls you, Nicolette. Her friend, Nicolette. Her professor, Nicolette, from St. David University. Nicolette the priest. Nicolette the teacher who thinks she should go to cook's school. Nicolette this, and Nicolette that. Nicolette the lover, who doesn't love her."

The color drains from Nikki's face, and her hands start to get clammy and sweat. "I can explain about Barrett. That was all a misunderstanding. I never meant to hurt or mislead her...."

Trang has a smirk on her face. "I never put this Nicolette together with Barnes. I don't think Barrett ever mentioned your last name. And a woman priest—I should have remembered how they called you 'Rev.'" She puts the rim of the glass to her lips, holds it there for a minute, but doesn't drink. "Saigon was so long ago. I never thought I would ever see you again. I didn't even know if you were alive. But...I did think about you."

She sips again and goes on. "Barrett, my very American child, was and still is, very much in love with you. She told me all about you when I returned from my last business trip to Vietnam. She let her father tell me about his decision to allow her go to that Culinary Institute. I didn't want her to be a common cook. I wanted something more, something better for both of my children."

She stands, walks to the bar and makes herself another drink.

Nikki regains some composure and pulls the overstuffed chair close to the table, then sits facing the sofa. Trang returns and again sits on the sofa, facing Nikki, who feels obligated to defend herself.

"I think Barrett will be an excellent chef. She has talent and interest in creating with her cooking." She pauses. "Barrett didn't like University work. She didn't always...," Nikki struggles for the right words.

"Fit in?" Trang finishes the sentence. "She never fit in. She fought everyone, dressed like a clown, was belligerent, disobeyed and rebelled constantly." Trang looks right at Nikki. "I know my children and love them for who they are. I push them so they will be able to take care of themselves. I know how hard this world can be."

Nikki maintains eye contact, trying to be perfectly clear. "I was never in love with Barrett. I never touched her, and I never knew she was your daughter."

Trang laughs softly and sits back on the sofa. Her laugh finally breaks the tension. "You must have almost died when you saw the picture of her mother—and she was me." She laughs again. This time with more feeling.

"I felt so much emotion, I had to run out of your

house and drive away." Nikki isn't laughing.

"I started to cry, Trang. I was so happy you and the baby made it out. I'd been carrying your picture for all those years, just hoping and praying that you were both all right."

Nikki gets her wallet out of the inside pocket of her navy-blue blazer. She shuffles through small pieces of paper and brings out an old, folded photo. She walks to the sofa and hands the photo to Trang.

Trang unfolds the photo and looks at the picture. "My baby, Celine." Trang rubs her finger over the photo, as if she can feel the baby. "She was so tiny then, and she cried all the time. I could not spend much time with her, and my uncle, who watched her...he had such pain of his own." She looks up at Nikki and says, "Did you realize, she's twenty-five now?"

Nikki nods her head, and Trang returns the photo to her. Nikki then sits on the sofa next to Trang and says, "I met Celine at the dinner Barrett had at your house while you were on the business trip. Celine is very beautiful."

"I hope she didn't fall in love with you too." Trang says sarcastically.

"No. She didn't!" Nikki tries to sound serious. "And I'm sure Barrett realizes I am in a relationship with someone, and she needs to stop this infatuation she has for me. Is Barrett the reason you wanted to see me?"

Trang hesitates before she answers. "No. Barrett tells me she will always love you. And I can actually see why." She pauses, sipping the bourbon slowly. "I have not told my daughters what I did to support myself in Saigon. Just that we met there. I did your cleaning, and you gave me the money to get to Malaysia. I don't like to talk about that part of my life."

"I don't talk about those times either...I think I'll have some water." Nikki gets up and goes to the bar for a glass of water. She looks up at Trang and says. "You don't have to worry about my saying anything to your daughters. As for Barrett, I'm sure she'll meet someone and forget about me...and what do you mean you can see why?" She returns to the chair and sits.

"You've grown quite charming. And the religious thing, that's made you more gentle, maybe a little sophisticated." Trang's voice seems to float with inflection, as if she's reading poetry.

Nikki stares at her again. "You're full of shit!" She says, starting to laugh. "You're telling me what you think I want to hear. But you don't have to flatter me. I already gave you the three thousand, and I didn't even have money like that then."

Trang laughs too. "Maybe you have gotten sophisticated. I see it will be harder to seduce you now."

"You never seduced me!" Nikki shoots back.

"Yes, but I did." Trang's eyes seem to hold Nikki's attention. "You gave me the money. You gave me the whiskey to sell. You took me on as your Mama San and paid me more than any other there."

"That was out of guilt!" Nikki is adamant now. "You didn't seduce me. I almost killed you. I...." There's suddenly a catch in Nikki's throat. "I...never could tell you. But...Trang...I'm so sorry for that day, for what I almost did. I never thought I'd get the chance to ask for your forgiveness. I never thought...."

Trang stands suddenly and walks to the window. Her back to Nikki, she looks out and says, "I hated you as much as you hated me. You were just another American soldier."

She turns back to Nikki. "And don't think that when you fell asleep, and I had that gun in my hand, that killing you didn't run through my mind. But I wasn't sure I'd get away with murder, and my baby needed me."

She walks back and stands in front of Nikki's chair. "And my baby needs me now. That's why I called. I need your help."

Nikki looks up at her. "What's wrong? How can I help you?"

Trang goes back to the sofa and sits down. They are eye level again. "Celine is in a great deal of trouble. I think her life is in danger."

"But, what can I do?" Nikki asks. "Have you gone to the police?"

Trang pushes her petite body back against the cushions of the sofa. She looks at her hands and explains, "Celine and I were fighting about many things. I wanted her to go back to college and come into the family business, perhaps take over as CEO someday. I wanted her to stop wasting her time making cheap jewelry and partying every night with her low class friends."

She looks up at Nikki. "She disappeared about three months ago. I waited for two days, but she never contacted me. I called everyone I could think of—even some of those friends. No one saw her. No one knew where she might be. They told me she had new friends they didn't know."

Trang stops talking, picks up the drink and sips. "After a whole week without hearing from her, I went to the police." Anger is apparent in her voice. "They couldn't help me. They said she was of age, probably wanted to get away from her parents...would turn up again when she ran out of money." She pauses again. "They were no help. They practically laughed at me. So, I went to my husband, Douglas. He was as worried as I, and we hired the best detective we could afford. He came here from New York City with access to all kinds of computer data and resources."

Her voice fades off as she again rubs the drink glass across her lips.

Nikki feels the tension in her silence and asks, "Did he find her?"

Trang moves the glass away from her lips. "Yes. He found her right across the border, right in Fort Erie, Canada. Only about twenty miles from here—but they might as well be a million miles."

"Why? What happened?" Nikki asks.

"Celine is working in a bar called, The Sin Club.

She...dances. The owner is her boyfriend, Joe Buglio. Have you heard of him?"

The name is all too familiar to Nikki—familiar to anyone who followed the sensationalized trial of six local mobsters. Buglio was one of the six. All were acquitted of dealing in drugs and prostitution, and conspiracy. "I remember the name from the trial," Nikki answers. "How did she get involved with him?"

"Celine used to go to Canada with her cocaine friends. Oh yes, I knew they used cocaine. I didn't think she did. Why would she? She was my talented, beautiful, intelligent daughter." Her voice catches for a moment. "I overheard her talking about the dance clubs and the male stripper bars. I thought it was harmless. She must have met Buglio at the club he owns."

Nikki interrupts. "If the detective found her, why didn't he bring her home?"

Trang looks directly at Nikki now. "She wouldn't come home. And he wouldn't take any amount of money I offered to make her come home. He didn't want anything to do with Buglio or the people he works for."

Nikki sees the pain in Trang's eyes, and asks, "But what can I do?"

"I know she wants to come home." Trang is pleading. "I know Buglio won't let her. I'm afraid of the drugs, afraid of what she's doing in that club. I went there and tried to see her, but when I asked for her, I was told to leave. She can't see me, and I can't even call her. Whoever answers the club phone just hangs up on me, or says Celine is not there."

Tears flow down her cheeks, as she starts to cry. Nikki moves to the sofa, and awkwardly takes Trang into her arms. Trang sobs soft, mournful tears, but only for a few short minutes. She chokes back her crying and composes herself, lifting her head quickly from Nikki's shoulder. She wipes her eyes with her hands, and plaintively says, "You must help me, Nikki. Please! I don't know who else to ask."

Trang's face is close to Nikki's, as she practically whispers. "Celine is still my baby—my Vietnam baby. I must help her."

Nikki feels her heart melting with sorrow for Trang's situation, and with sadness for the Amerasian girl who's in trouble. She feels herself being pulled by Trang's eyes into the very soul of this woman...feels the same pull she felt years ago in NAM—and this feeling scares her enough to remove her arms from the comforting embrace and lean away from Trang. "What do you want me to do?"

Trang inches closer, saying, "Just go to The Sin Club. Try to see Celine, just talk to her. If she wants to come home, and I know she does, then...." She stops talking, not finishing the sentence.

"And if she wants to come home, then what?" Nikki wants Trang to finish her sentence.

Trang looks at Nikki again and answers, "Then I want you to get her out of there, away from that club, away from that man."

"I don't know if I can do this." Nikki breaks Trang's stare by standing up. "I'm not sure about even how to do this. I need to think for a minute." She goes to the window and looks down at the water.

Trang is behind her, then next to her, looking at the water too. "You can do it, Nikki. You're the only one who can." She touches Nikki's arm and pulls her attention away from the water. "Please, do this for me. If you care about me at all. Do this for me and for Celine."

Nikki puts her arms around Trang's shoulders and draws her closer. "I'll try Trang. You know I'll do whatever I can to help you save your war baby. I feel like I owe you this much."

Trang sinks further into the embrace. Her face is almost buried in Nikki's blazer when she pushes slowly away saying, "I knew you'd help me. I knew you would."

Nikki turns and looks out the window at the water

again. Through the mist coming off the lake, she can see a blurry outline of the Canadian shoreline. She thinks out loud, "I can go to Buglio's club in the evening. She's more likely to be there then. I don't know if she'll recognize me, but I'll tell her who I am. Remind her of our meeting at Barrett's dinner."

She stops devising her plan for a minute and turns back to Trang, asking, "What happened to Celine?"

Trang walks slowly to the bar for a refill. She looks up at Nikki and tries to explain. "Celine, my little Truong, finally stopped crying while we were in Malaysia. After I met Douglas, I spent every moment with my baby...she was still happy when we came to America, to Buffalo. She grew up in the house we still live in."

Trang walks back to the windows. Staring out at nothing and continues, "Things began to change when she became a teenager. She looked different. That's what she told me. She looked black but she felt Asian. I did try to teach her a little about Vietnam, my parents, some of our customs. Not very much. You see, I wanted her to be American. I knew that's how she would succeed. But Celine felt different from her classmates, and it was very important for her to be like the other Americans."

Trang turns from the window and stares across the room. "Did you know, she won a full scholarship to Boston University. She is very intelligent, but she turned it down. Studied instead at some storefront art co-op. She wanted to design jewelry. Her friends, if you can call them that, are all anti-social, spoiled children, bored with everything. None of them have employment. They live mostly off their parent's money. They convinced Celine that she was just like them. They convinced her that she should abandon the life her parents were forcing on her. They said I didn't see her as she really was. She needed to do her own thing. That's how she put it to me. She needed to do her own thing.'"

Trang sips from her drink, still staring into space.

"I didn't think I was forcing anything on her. I didn't want her to be different. It's too difficult to be different. She really is very artistic. I can see the talent in the pieces she gave me. But I want more for her. I want her to use her full potential, to be confident, self-sufficient. Is that so bad?" She turns to Nikki with this last question.

"What if she won't come home?" Nikki asks directly.

Trang's eyes lock onto Nikki's again, as she answers, "Tell her I love her. I won't force her to do anything she doesn't want to do. I will support her...she can make her jewelry at home...or I'll rent a studio. Anything she wants."

"What about the drugs?" Nikki asks, trying to get as much information as she needs. "Is she very involved with drugs?"

"I don't know...she may be," Trang's voice expresses her fear of what might be. "Some of her friends were arrested for possession of cocaine. I asked her, but she never really answered me." Her voice fades off. "I never wanted to know the answer. I was afraid."

Nikki gives Trang a half-smile and tries to lay out the rest of her plan. "Once I can talk to her, I'll tell her you just want to know that she's okay. I'll tell her you just want to see her and talk to her. I'll bring her back with me, or..." She wants Trang to realize there may be different outcomes. "Or I will try to set up a meeting between you two."

Nikki lowers her voice, as the reality of the situation lowers her own confidence. "That's probably the only thing I can do, Trang."

Trang puts her hand on Nikki's arm, sending an unexpected shiver through Nikki's entire body. Trang smiles a sad smile and says, "Celine knows you saved our lives. She will trust you like I trust you. She will come home with you."

Nikki decides to leave with this positive thought rather than the many negative thoughts about this situation, now racing through her head. She declines Trang's invitation to stay for lunch, explaining she has to meet Ginni, Dr.

Virginia Clayton, her partner. Ginni's attending a medical lecture at the Convention Center, a few blocks away.

Nikki walks to the room door, ready to leave. She turns back to say goodbye and again sees Trang as the teenage mother of an Amerasian child...working the streets of Saigon...and now...standing alone in this large, empty hotel room.

Nikki says, "I have to go now. But, I'll call you tomorrow and let you know when I'm going to Fort Erie."

Trang gives her a weak wave, and Nikki closes the door behind her. This last image of Trang stays in her mind, as she takes the elevator down to the lobby, goes to her car, and drives to the Convention Center.

CHAPTER 2

Late spring brings daily, light drizzles to Western New York. Buffalo is no exception. Nikki, still preoccupied, weaves through the one-way streets listening to the thump, thump of her car wipers. Visually scanning the curbside for a parking spot, she sees Ginni waiting on the sidewalk outside the Convention Center. Ginni's red blazer is pulled tightly around her with one hand, and an open umbrella is in the other. Nikki pulls up to the curb, and Ginni closes the umbrella, sliding into the passenger seat. Nikki maneuvers the car back into traffic.

"How was the lecture?" Nikki asks rather preoccupied with her own thoughts.

Ginni gives Nikki a long look, which Nikki doesn't return. Instead, she continues intently driving, not really interested or paying attention to Ginni.

"The lecture was helpful, especially for my work at the hospice. New treatments for AIDS are turning up almost monthly and many have been documented as extending life up to two years." Ginni answers clinically.

"That's good." Nikki mutters.

"How was your lunch with Trang?" Ginni asks, getting right to the point.

Nikki hesitates a little too long before answering. "I didn't really get any lunch."

"I thought you were meeting for lunch." Ginni's green eyes widen, as she militantly pushes on. "What restaurant did you go to?"

Nikki takes her left hand off the wheel and combs her fingers through the top of her short, curly hair, again. "We didn't go to a restaurant....Trang reserved a room at the hotel."

Ginni takes a noticeable pause before speaking again. "Really! Now let me see if I have this right. Trang, the ex-prostitute and your Mama-San from Vietnam, whose daughter turns out to be your student, a student madly in love with you. This is the Trang who rented a hotel room for your reunion." Her irritation is apparent in the red hue that suddenly appears on her dark skinned cheeks. The sarcasm of her speech also conveys her latent anger. "Did you know about the hotel room, Nikki? Did you know that's where you were meeting?"

"No!" Nikki throws her a quick look. "We were supposed to meet in the lobby and go to a restaurant. She changed the plan because of what she wanted to talk about. We had a very sensitive discussion, and she didn't want to be in a public place."

Ginni tries to control her rising anger by carefully pronouncing each word. "Did...this... sensitive discussion...involve any touching."

"No!" Nikki looks at her again. "What's wrong with you. You know I always wondered if Trang and her baby escaped. I told you all about them when we first met."

Ginni tries to calm her reaction. "And I always heard more than just concern in your voice, Nikki, whenever you talked about Trang. There was this big unfinished something in your voice."

"I don't know what you're talking about." Nikki

hunts for an explanation. "There was never anything between Trang and me except that unfortunate business with the gun, when I almost killed her. I just felt guilty after that."

"I didn't always hear guilt. There was more caring than guilt." Ginni's red cheeks have returned to their natural olive-skinned color, but she still fidgets, playing with the three earrings in her left earlobe. "How could you just go up to a hotel room with her? You haven't seen her in over twenty-five years?"

Nikki looks for an available parking spot, pulls over, and turns off the car. "What is this all about? I went up to the room with her because she needed to talk. Her daughter's in trouble, and she needs my help. Why are you so angry about this?"

Ginni leans into Nikki's face now. "I'm angry and pissed, because I'm jealous! Is that so hard for you to understand? I don't like you in hotel rooms with attractive Asians. I saw her picture in the newspaper. She's a wealthy and successful business woman, and she's very pretty, Nikki. And I'm jealous!" She finally drops back into her seat.

Nikki doesn't know how to answer this last outburst. She unfastens her seat belt and leans over to Ginni. "You don't have to be jealous. You don't have to worry about me in hotel rooms or at meetings with pretty women." She lowers her voice and moves closer. "I love you, Ginni," she says, kissing her tenderly on the lips.

Ginni puts her arms around Nikki's neck and kisses back. "I'm sorry. I guess all the sad stuff in the AIDS lecture got me feeling insecure. I love you too."

Nikki smiles at her and moves back to the driver's seat, where she fastens the seat belt again. She starts the car and pulls out into the street. She's about to say something, when Ginni quietly adds. "But she is pretty, and you care about her."

Nikki nods her head up and down in exasperation. "Yes. She's pretty, always was, and I care about her.

One of the reasons I always cared about her is

because an American soldier used her and left her with an Amerasian child to raise. And she is desperate now to save that child."

Ginni is finally comfortable changing the subject. "What kind of trouble is she in, Nikki? How can you help her?"

Nikki's also glad to move on to another subject. "Celine is involved with drugs and some mobster up in Canada. She disappeared a few months ago. Trang hired a detective who found Celine, but he wouldn't try to bring her home. He's afraid of the mobster."

"And you're not afraid of him, right!" Ginni is raising her voice again. "Nikki, I thought you weren't going to get involved in things like this. This sounds dangerous."

"I won't get involved in anything dangerous." Nikki tries to explain. "I'm just going to work something out so I can see Celine and ask her if she wants to come home. That's all I'm going to do."

"That's too much to try and do." Ginni quickly replies. "And it's dangerous!"

"I don't even have a plan yet!" Now Nikki raises her voice. "Once I have a plan, I promise, I'll run it past you for approval. Will that get you to stop worrying?"

Ginni is now reserved and controlled. "Yes, that will be acceptable. And I appreciate your including me in situations which affect your safety." She puts her hands in her lap.

Nikki is shaking her head again, but this time she's smiling. She reaches over and puts her hand on top of Ginni's. "I do love you."

Ginni looks at their intertwined hands and says, "Me too."

Nikki removes her hand from Ginni's, so she can grab the steering wheel for a sharp left turn. "What time did you tell Magpie we'd pick her up?"

Nikki is shaking her head again, but this time she's smiling. She reaches over and puts her hand on top of Ginni's. "I do love you."

Ginni looks at their intertwined hands and says, "Me too."

Nikki removes her hand from Ginni's, so she can grab the steering wheel for a sharp left turn. "What time did you tell Magpie we'd pick her up?"

"Her name is Mary." Ginni says, looking at her watch. "And I told her we'd be there about thirty minutes ago."

"If she can call me 'Leftenant', I can call her Magpie. Anyway, I think she likes the nickname. Anything to remind her of the war. You know, the war to end all wars. The one she insists on constantly talking about."

"Mary talks about the Falklands War because it still affects her," Ginni tries to justify Mary's behavior. "Mary was only twenty-three when she went to the Falklands. That's young for a London Associated Press photographer. And remember, that war was never in her career plans. Mary studied painting at the Royal Academy of Art. That was during the same years that Linda Kitson taught there. I think Mary was very impressed by Kitson's work, especially her London Time's exhibit of Fleet Street and the world of reporting. Mary wanted to somehow follow in Kitson's footsteps."

"Kitson was that war correspondent, right?" Nikki asks.

"Not a correspondent," Ginni corrects Nikki. "Linda Kitson was the first British woman to be an official war artist. She was selected by the Imperial War Museum Committee; even given honorary officer status. Kitson is history now, the only British woman allowed to participate in the war."

Ginni listens for a moment to the rhythmic windshield wipers, before she goes on. "Mary was fascinated when she read about Kitson going over to record the war through her art. It was several years after Mary finished her record the war in an artistic way. She was terribly unprepared for what was going on over there." Ginni looks over at Nikki, who listens intently while she drives.

"She's feeling some of the same things you felt when you got back from Vietnam, and she's having some of the same nightmares you still have," Ginni adds.

Nikki throws her a quick look, and says, "She wasn't a soldier; she was a photographer. And that war only lasted three months."

"But Mary was right in the heart of the fighting," Ginni explains. "She saw most of the battles. Vietnam was at least a modern war. The Falklands was more like World War I. When Mary arrived there in early May, it was winter. She said the weather was awful, freezing temperatures. Most of the land was just mud and bogs. The Falkland Islands are just a bunch of sheep farms, I guess."

Ginni takes a long, deliberate breath before she continues, "No vehicles could get through that mud, so the British soldiers had to carry huge packs with their mortars, rifles, machine guns, and anti-tank rockets all strapped to their backs. And the fighting was often hand to hand, bayonet to bayonet. Mary slogged through that mud with those soldiers, and she took close-up pictures of those men and the Argentine soldiers...killing each other."

Nikki pulls into a parking spot outside the Metro Bus Terminal, turns off the car, and says quietly, "I do understand what she went through. I didn't mean to sound impatient with Magpie...and she likes that name because the Welsh Guards gave it to her. She probably talked non-stop whenever she was with them."

Ginni unfastens her seat belt. "At least she talks about her war. At least she tries to deal with what happened to her. Which is more than I can say about some old soldiers."

Nikki ignores the obvious reference to herself. They both get out of the car and walk together into the terminal.

CHAPTER 3

The large bus station is busy for early afternoon. The five-year-old terminal is expansive and bright with full windows on three sides of the huge room. At opposite ends of the back wall are two lines of about a dozen people each, purchasing tickets. There are about thirty rows of plastic seats attached back to back on either side of a middle mall of security offices and a gift shop. Some of the seats are autographed with graffiti, half-smudged by the cleaning persons, who work continuously to remove it.

Small groups and couples are here and there causing a quiet buzzing of conversation. A larger group of about six people sit in the farthest corner on the left side of the room. Louder, more animated conversation seems to be buzzing from this group.

Both Nikki and Ginni scan the right side of the terminal, looking down rows of seats, trying to spot Magpie. They start walking across the bus station, working their way back to the glass doors, and then moving down the left side.

"There she is!" Ginni points to the animated group at the end of the room. "I think that's Mary!"

Nikki can't be sure at first, but as they walk closer to the gathering, she confirms Ginni's identification. There's Magpie, her legs tucked under her small boned, five-foot frame. Her arms gesticulating wildly. She's holding court, talking non-stop as usual. Everyone's attention is fixed on her. Not even aware of what she is doing, Magpie verbally never gives even one of the listeners a chance to jump into the conversation.

As Ginni and Nikki approach the rapt audience, Magpie spots them. "Ginni!" She unfolds her legs and jumps off the chair in what appears to be one move.

"Ginni!" Magpie runs up to Ginni. "I'm so glad to see you. It seems like years since the last time I was here. I thought I had the arrival time wrong, so I just kept asking different people what time it was, and what do you know we got into a conversation. The bus ride down seemed to take forever. I'm glad I brought something with me to eat and something to read. You know I have no patience for sitting that long." She must take a breath, giving Ginni time to respond by giving her a big hug.

"I'm glad to see you too," Ginni says, breaking the embrace. "I think it's just over a year since we saw you last."

Magpie stays in the half-embrace. "Has it been over a year? Let me think, I guess it has. You took that art course from me at the gallery about five years ago, that's when we met. And I came down to Buffalo for lunch a few times, but that was before Aunt Geneva got sick. And the last time I came down was for the wedding. Well, I mean it wasn't a wedding really, but the party with your family and friends, where you introduced everyone to Nikki....Oh. Hi, Nikki!"

She leaves Ginni's arms and goes to Nikki, giving her a quick hug. "Good to see you too. You look well. It was really nice of you to drive all the way here and to invite me to stay with you two."

She walks the few steps back to Ginni. "Let me just get my bag and say goodbye to these people. I'll be right back."

She returns to the gathering, shakes hands with all of the people there, talking non-stop. Then she picks up a large canvas duffle-bag, slings the strap over her shoulder, and walks back toward Nikki and Ginni.

Nikki moves closer to Ginni and whispers. "She's been drinking. I can smell the whiskey. I'll bet she didn't eat anything on the bus ride, just drank her way down from Toronto."

"Shhh!" Ginni gives Nikki a harsh look and whispers, "Let her alone for now. I'll try and explain everything to you when we get home." She softens. "Please, she's my friend, try to be nice to her."

"Well, I must be carrying bricks in this thing." Magpie is next to them now. "I always meant to buy one of those fancy suitcases. You know, maybe one with a designer logo on it, but I never seem to get around to making the purchase. Would you believe this is the same bag I had when I left England to move in with my Aunt in Toronto? And that must be at least ten years ago...."

Ginni smiles at Magpie, putting an arm around her. Then she directs her toward the door where the car is parked. Nikki can see that the duffle-bag if stood on end would be almost as tall as Magpie, so she steps closer to them and says, "Let me take your bag for you."

"Oh, that's sweet of you, Leftenant." Magpie lets the shoulder strap slide off. "I can usually handle it all right, but I'm feeling a little tired today."

Nikki takes the bag and swings the strap over her shoulder. The bag does feel like there are bricks inside. She shares a knowing glance with Ginni, a soft and tender look that reminds Nikki of how much she cares for her partner.

They make their way through the terminal and out the double doors to the street. Ginni and Magpie are arm in arm. Magpie is weaving a bit in her walk and jabbers on even faster as the cool air hits her.

Magpie insists on sitting in the back seat, where she continues talking to the back of both Nikki's and Ginni's heads.

There's a sudden moment of silence in the back seat. Both Nikki and Ginni think Magpie may be asleep. She isn't asleep, but her drunkenness and drowsiness have caused her mind to make abrupt changes in thought patterns.

"I tripped over a blown-off leg and fell next to a helmet with a human head still in it." Magpie's speech has slowed down considerably. "Did I ever tell you about that, Ginni? Two of us, a bloke from the Independent Television News and me, hitched a ride on a Sea King helicopter from the base camp, Port San Carlos. It was the main settlement of the island, a 97,709 acre sheep farm with a population of 30 people, including 10 children. We were headed to Goose Green, one of the bloodiest battlefields of the whole Falklands War. Some of the boys there had been fighting for several weeks already. It was cold; the average temperature was 37 degrees. My fingers were so numb, sometimes I couldn't even push down the button on my camera. And the humidity was always high. A sleety rain fell everyday. The land was all muddy pastures and soggy marshes."

"The first things we came across were the Scorpion light tanks, jeeps, anti-aircraft missiles, and light artillery, all stuck in the muddy ooze. I took a few dozen rolls of film there. We slogged a bit farther, heading for a cluster of white stone buildings that used to be the village. Bodies and parts of bodies were everywhere. Next to them were rifles and backpacks, even unexploded shells. They were all stuck in this dark mud pudding."

There's a long moment of silence again, and Nikki looks at Ginni who puts her finger to her lips, silencing any remark Nikki may have thought of making. Magpie lets out a deep sigh and continues talking. "I don't think I told you this part, Ginni. Our helicopter pilot warned us to be careful where we walked. A regiment of Gurkhas was already there trying to clear the area of bombs. So, when I stepped down from the helicopter, I was carrying two bags of my camera equipment and film. I had my Pentax around my neck and a small Nikkon in the left pocket of my photographer's vest, which I wore over my long, wool coat. I also had a heavy, folded tripod under my arm. But, I was in good shape then. Hell, I was only in my twenties, and I did some long-distance running. I was running three to four miles each day after work. Not like today, when I can't even lift my own duffle bag."

She stops again, pensively thinking out loud, "I only took a few steps when I tripped over the leg. I fell right down in that mud, eye to eye with the helmet with the head in it. I think it was one of their soldiers...the Argentines. I felt trapped in all that ooze. I couldn't get up because the mud was like quicksand. I tried to stand and fell back down. That's when I hit my forehead on a piece of shrapnel that was stuck there." Her voice lowers. "I still have the scar."

Nikki watches Magpie through the rear-view mirror. She rubs the faint scar just above her eye. Nikki again looks at Ginni, whose pained expression for her friend's suffering, touches Nikki's emotions too.

Ginni turns her head and says to Magpie, "Just how did that whole war happen, Mary? What was the Falklands War all about, anyway?"

Magpie tries to get enthusiastic again, but tiredness is apparent in her voice. "The Falklands War was really an attempt by the military junta in Argentina to distract the Argentines from their internal problems, like their declining economy and high unemployment. The rallying cry, however, was a five-hundred year dispute over who really owns those God-forsaken Islands. The whole group of islands only has about 1800 inhabitants and most of them are British sheep farmers."

Magpie's voice grows heavier as she goes on. "An English explorer named John Davis claimed the Falklands in 1592. But, since there are 200 islands, they were settled over the following years by both the English and Spanish."

Magpie yawns and talks at the same time, "In the seventeen hundreds, French colonists settled on East Falkland and the Spanish bought them out. Then there was the English-Spanish War, and the English said they would leave the islands."

"But, by the eighteen hundreds, Argentina won independence from Spain and claimed all Spanish land in its surrounding area, including the Falklands. The English returned in 1833 and claimed them too."

Magpie now sounds like she's reciting from a textbook, "During World War II, Argentina claimed to be neutral but by the end of the war helped supply the allies. In exchange for their alliance, Britain did discuss giving ownership to Argentina, but nothing was settled. The United Nations began negotiations to settle the dispute in the 1960's, and talks were still going on in 1982."

Magpie coughs, interrupting her ongoing commentary. She shakes away some of her drowsiness and begins again, "It was April 2, 1982 when Argentine President Leopoldo Galtieri, landed thousands of troops on the Falkland Islands and reclaimed them as Islas Malvinas. Margaret Thatcher, our Prime Minister at the time, deployed a naval task force, and on May 21, thousands of British Marines and paratroopers landed in the Falklands. And the rest is history...." Magpie is silent again.

This time, Ginni unfastens her seat belt and turns all the way around to check on Magpie. Turning back, she fastens her belt again and quietly says to Nikki, "She's asleep."

Nikki has another twenty miles to drive before they reach their townhouse in Sheridan, New York. She takes another look in the rearview mirror. Magpie's small frame and features make her resemble a little girl who has finally fallen asleep on the long ride home.

CHAPTER 4

"She has a drinking problem." Nikki says impatiently. "Since I've known her, she's always half drunk. And she's really in the bag tonight. I bet by morning she won't remember a thing about how we practically carried her into the guest room and put her to bed."

"Shhh! Keep your voice down." Ginni's on the defensive, her green eyes flashing. "Of all people, Nikki Barnes, I expect you to be more sympathetic. You know what it's like to go through a war. And even if you've forgotten what the alienation felt like when you returned home—I know you haven't forgotten what you saw and what you experienced over there. Well, Mary went through the same things."

Nikki punches the pillow propped up behind her and leans back further on the headboard. "I know. I really do know. It's just that...I don't want to be reminded of it all. Seeing her and listening to her stories is like all my old scars opening up and bleeding again. I'm not really angry at her. I'm angry at what happened to the two of us...angry at war, I guess."

Ginni moves closer and gives her a peck on the cheek. Still resting her hands on Nikki's arm, she says. "That's not the only reason she's drinking again." Ginni sits back. "When you first met her at our reception, her Aunt Geneva had just been diagnosed with the cancerous brain tumor. The irony is, Mary's decision to live in Toronto with her Aunt was based on her fear that she could become an alcoholic, if she didn't leave England and all the war memories there."

Ginni sits up straight before continuing, "She knew she was drinking too much when she returned to London after the Falklands. She couldn't deal with the flashbacks or the uncontrollable crying. She told me about the nightmares, waking up screaming and crying. The whiskey bottle was her only relief and that scared her too."

Nikki silently nods her head, remembering the same crying and nightmares, and the friends who drowned all the pain with booze or drugs.

"Mary thought the invitation from her Aunt was just what she needed." Ginni looks for a moment at the wall separating the guest room from theirs. "Geneva was an artist herself, mostly seascapes, I think. She had her own studio in her house and a spare bedroom. Mary could use the studio and do some of her own paintings. Which she did. That's when she started the flower series. She told me she would go days, even weeks, without a drink."

"Then Geneva started getting dizzy episodes and passing out. Mary became her caretaker. The cancer moved very quickly because there wasn't much that could be done." Ginni pauses for a moment before continuing.

"When Geneva died, she left the house and most of her belongings to Mary. That's why Mary stayed. And she did put more and more time and energy into her paintings. She had some gallery showings and got good critical reviews...but the loss was too much for her—she started drinking again. And I don't think she's been able to stop. She still lives all alone up there. I think her agent's the only person she really socializes with." Ginni's voice fades off.

Nikki gets Ginni's attention back by asking, "Is that why she's here? Are you going to help her stop drinking?"

Ginni reaches over and takes Nikki's hand. "No, that's not the reason." She leans in closer and almost whispering says, "And I know I don't have to say this, but it's strictly confidential. Mary's been having headaches and dizzy spells. It may be nothing, but since she was coming to Buffalo for the gallery display, she asked if I could check her out medically. I think she's scared she might have a tumor too."

Nikki reaches over and envelops Ginni in her arms. She kisses her on the lips, first softly with all the love and tenderness she feels for her right now. She kisses her again; this time with more passion. Ginni kisses back. Their lips speak an unheard but known language. Tongues move in and out, touching and exploring in a ballet of slippery searching. Ginni's hands find the buttons on Nikki's loose pajama top. With little effort, she unfastens each one while still in the embrace.

Nikki moves her hands to the bottom of Ginni's scrub top, gently lifting it over her head. In unison they come together again, kissing, searching with more passion. They slide further under the covers, down from the headboard, flat on the bed, arms and legs entwined, bare breasts to bare breasts, heat rising in both of them. Skin to skin, Nikki's hands feel every inch of Ginni's back. She can count most of her ribs, blindly touch every mole and mark.

Nikki's hands work their way down Ginni's back to her waist—moving her open palms back and forth, she sculpts Ginni as if for the first time. Reaching the elastic on Ginni's scrub pants, Nikki loops her thumbs in the waistband. One on each side. She slowly starts to pull the pants down.

Still kissing, they both breathe heavier and heavier. The pants are just about to finish their slow ride over Ginni's hips, when Ginni pulls away from the kissing.

"Nikki, no! We can't!" Ginni's loud whisper forces Nikki's hands to pull up the pants.

"Why? What's wrong?" Nikki's arousal from her

contact with Ginni's skin, gives her the incentive to try pushing the pants back down.

Ginni stops her hand again. But this time she leans in and kisses Nikki's chest before she quietly says. "Mary is right in the other room. You know how thin these walls are."

Nikki stops fighting for the pants. Instead, she brings her arms back around Ginni, holding her close so that their breasts form a row of hills and valleys. "Magpie was very asleep when she hit the bed. I don't think she'll hear anything."

"But what if she does?" Ginni is serious, sincerely worried.

Nikki tries to reassure her. "What if she does? I'm sure she'll figure out what we're doing and go back to sleep."

"Nikki!" Ginni pushes away from the embrace and searches for her scrub top. "I don't want Mary hearing me make love to you."

"I think she's figured out that we do it," Nikki says, the ardor quickly leaving the room.

Ginni finishes putting on the top. "Maybe she has, but you know how the British are. I think we need to behave with a sense of propriety. She is a guest."

"Propriety!" Nikki says out loud. "This is our house. It's perfectly normal...maybe you're just worried because you think she isn't getting any, and you don't want her to feel bad."

"Keep your voice down!" Ginni's face now matches the red highlights in her hair. She starts to exchange barb with barb, but changes her mind. She calms down and smiles, saying. "Maybe you're right."

She puts her hand on Nikki's lips, silencing any further protests, and helps her get back into her loose pajama top. Ginni buttons the four buttons, kissing Nikki after each one.

Nikki knows Ginni well enough to realize this

discussion is over. She lingers a little longer on the last kiss. Then she punches down her pillow, lies down and rolls over, her back to Ginni.

Ginni fluffs up her pillow, then lies down close enough to Nikki to wrap her arm around Nikki's waist. Their bodies conform to the same curves, with Ginni's face resting on Nikki's back, as she says. "Good night, Nikki. I love you."

Nikki lets her arm rest on Ginni's arm which is wrapped around her in a hug. "Me too. Good night."

�֍

Ginni and Nikki watch Mary Magpie York pad barefoot into their airy and bright townhouse kitchen. Her fine, shoulder-length hair is disheveled, forming billowy, slightly closed curtains on either side of her face. Her puffy eyelids almost hide her sparkling brown eyes. She wears a white, ripped sweatshirt with the arms cut off and blue cotton briefs. Rubbing her tangled hair, she says, "Morning, Leftenant. Why are you dressed like the vicar?"

Her appearance and casual remark cause Ginni to laugh and choke on her half-swallowed coffee. She ends up spitting it across the table toward Nikki, who quickly pulls back to avoid the spray.

Magpie rubs her temples now, as she addresses Ginni. "Would you have any aspirin, Ginni? I can't seem to find mine, and my head is breaking. Must be the change in temperature, or maybe I ate something bad, or I slept wrong, although the mattress in that room is just fine...but my head...."

Ginni stands up immediately, and says, "I'll get some, right away. Why don't you sit there?" She points to the empty chair next to hers and heads for the medicine cabinet in the bathroom. Turning back for a moment, she adds, "Nikki will pour you some coffee?"

Nikki gives Ginni a bothered look but gets up, takes a mug from the cupboard and moves to the coffee maker.

Magpie braces herself at the chair, pulls it out gingerly, and slowly sits down. Nikki puts the steaming cup of coffee in front of Magpie and in an irritated tone asks, "Cream?"

Magpie notices the irritation and quietly answers, "No. Just black." She takes another long look at Nikki, who is right next to her now, and asks. "Is today Sunday?"

Nikki's impatience is obvious now, as she moves back to her own cup of coffee. She sits down, eye level with Magpie, and says, "I do Pastoral Counseling twice a week at the Haven of Hope Hospice in Niagara Falls. The people living there sometimes want to see a priest. The staff requested I wear my clerics today."

Magpie gives her a blank stare, then says, "And you can get away with that violet shirt?"

This makes even Nikki smile. She pulls at the bright colored clerical shirt, looking at the front of it. "They come in all colors now. I even have a red one."

Magpie smiles back and sips the hot coffee. Then she asks, "And the hospice doesn't mind that you're queer?"

Nikki is taken off guard by this last question, but she responds anyway. "The question of my being gay has never come up. But if it does, I never deny who I am. Plus, I don't think it will matter. Many of the patients at the hospice are gay men with HIV related illnesses."

Magpie blows gently at her coffee, trying to cool it off. She takes another sip and comments, "I never told anyone I was gay. My parents didn't want to know. They dropped enough hints about how they would die if their child was a queer. And the lads in the Falklands were so homophobic almost every other joke was about a fag. I could never be myself until I moved in with Aunt Geneva. She told me artists were allowed to be anything, as long as it was true to themselves...because that would show in their work."

Ginni returns to the kitchen at this point, gets a glass of water, and places the water and two aspirins in front of

Magpie. Putting her coffee cup down again, Magpie scoops up the pills, pops them in her mouth, and washes them down with the water. "Thanks. I needed that."

She pats Ginni's arm, as Ginni sits next to her. "And what's on your program for today?" Magpie asks.

Ginni cheerily answers, "I'm off to the Medical Center to see my standing list of patients. When Nikki gets home at four, she'll bring you over. I've scheduled you for last today."

Nikki does a double-take. It seems Ginni left the "driving her to the Medical Center part" out of their "Magpie Talk" last night.

"Nikki...I..." Ginni realizes her omission. "I forgot to ask you last night. Will you be able to bring Mary down to the Center? Can you fit it in? I can leave and come and get her, if you can't."

Nikki softens and smiles at her. "No problem." She turns to Magpie and jokes, "I'll be back promptly at four—so be ready, Magpie."

Magpie does a half-hearted salute. "Yes, Leftenant. I shall be in full medical exam uniform." She pauses for a second. "And just what is that, a paper robe, a sheet, or just skivvies?"

They all laugh, breaking any existing tension. Nikki and Ginni leave the house together heading for their respective cars. Just before they separate, Ginni reaches over, squeezes Nikki's hand, and says, "Thanks for understanding."

CHAPTER 5

Nikki isn't sure her plan to get Celine home, or at least to get her to meet with Trang, will work. She plays it out in her head several times on her drive back and forth to the hospice. She decides to call Trang when she gets to the townhouse and tell her she's going to Fort Erie tonight to try and see Celine.

As Nikki enters her living room, she sees Magpie sleeping soundly on the sofa. Nikki laughs quietly at Magpie's outfit. She wears worn jeans and a long-sleeved white blouse and uses her black leather aviator jacket as a blanket. Even stretched out, her small body only covers half the sofa.

Something suddenly touches Nikki deep inside her heart, as she watches Magpie sleep. It's the same feeling she gets whenever she watches a parade or visits the Vietnam War Memorial on the Buffalo waterfront. This military kinship, deep inside, causes a tear to trickle down her face. She feels the pain of a comrade, another soldier, a pain she immediately shares.

Walking over to the sofa, she kneels down and brushes the stray stands of hair away from Magpie's face. Then she gently touches her shoulder, waking her.

"It's almost time to go," Nikki says quietly.

Magpie wakes up slowly, covering a yawn with her

hand. She gives a two-finger salute, and says. "I'm dressed and ready, Sir!"

Nikki smiles and stands up again. "Take a few minutes to wake up. I have to change out of my Sunday suit and make a short phone call. Why don't you put on a pot of coffee, and we'll have a cup before we leave."

Nikki goes into the bedroom and changes into a black tee-shirt and jeans. Through her open bedroom door, she hears Magpie moving around in the kitchen. She sits on the edge of her bed with the portable phone and pushes Trang's number. The phone is picked up on the second ring, as if Trang was waiting for the call.

"I decided not to wait too long," Nikki tries to explain. "I'm just going to drive over there tonight and see if I can get in. They don't know me, so I figure I have a chance. Then, when I see Celine, I'll try and talk to her."

Trang's reply is short and cryptic. "Whatever you think, Nikki. Whatever you think will work. I want her home...and safe. Please get her out of there."

"I'll make sure I get to talk to her." Nikki feels that pain again. But this time, the sound of Trang's voice intensifies the feeling, as if it has been dislodged from a hidden memory and pushed quickly forward, all the ragged edges scraping along the sides of her heart. "I'm sure that once I explain how worried you are, she'll want to see you. And if she's being held against her will, I promise, Trang, I'll get her out of there. You'll have her back home as soon as I can arrange it, and no drugs, no mobster, no security guard is going to stop me."

In an emotionally controlled voice, Trang says, "Thank you again, Nikki. Goodbye."

Nikki slowly hangs up the receiver and gets off the bed to return the phone to the dresser. Turning from the dresser, she sees Magpie standing in the doorway.

"I wondered if you want decaf," Magpie says sheepishly, knowing she's been caught listening to the conversation. "I didn't mean to eavesdrop on your call." She pauses, feeling Nikki's *please explain why you were eavesdropping* stare. "I think you've got yourself a mission, Leftenant," Magpie continues. "I think you might need an enlisted man to come along on that one."

Nikki doesn't say anything for a few minutes, then answers, "Decaf sounds just fine." Crossing to the door, she forces Magpie to step aside while she exits.

In the kitchen, Nikki finishes making the coffee while Magpie talks to her back. "Mobsters and drugs doesn't sound like a night of fun." Magpie tries to sound nonchalant. "I can be a help...but who are we getting out?"

Nikki turns to her. "*We* are not getting anyone out. I have a friend who needs my help." She thinks a moment and adds, "And I'd appreciate it if you didn't say anything about this to Ginni."

"Of course." Magpie sits at the table. "She'd probably worry if she heard you were involved in something like this. It sounds dangerous. So, I won't tell her anything...." She looks directly at Nikki, and adds. "But I come along for backup. If not, and I hate to manipulate an officer Leftenant, but I come along or I tell her. She's my friend, and I know she wouldn't want you going alone. So it's me going, or her knowing, take your choice."

Nikki is so angry she considers grabbing Magpie by the back of her collar and tossing her across the room. Even though Nikki's only three inches taller than the five-foot Magpie, she outweighs her by a good forty pounds.

Magpie's small enough, so Nikki probably could toss her across the room. Instead, she considers the consequences of letting Magpie tell Ginni what she's planning to do in Fort Erie. Ginni would find a way to stop her, and she needs to do this for Trang. Against all her better judgment, she reluctantly says, "Okay, you can come along, but not a word to Ginni—not now; not ever. Is that clear?"

Magpie's on her feet. "Yes sir. I'm perfectly trained

for covert missions. Remember, according to all the public war records, I was never even in the Falklands. Press photographers were just civilians considered visiting at the time. I saw an awful lot of war for just a visitor. The Associated Press in London liked most of my photos, and they published about twenty. But no one in the press corps warned me about how the war would affect me and remain such a part of my life, and not a good part either."

Magpie catches herself wandering off the subject. "Your secret is safe with me. So, what's the plan?"

Over coffee, Nikki briefly describes the problem and the plan she has in mind.

"Sounds like we're mostly going to wing it, Leftenant." Magpie calmly states, as they get up to leave for the Medical Center.

"Fake it is what we tend to say over here." Nikki adds, as she opens the door.

"I'm ready for action." Magpie salutes again and heads for the car.

❁

Nikki leaves Magpie in Ginni's capable and friendly hands and walks back through the Memorial Medical Center entrance and down the path that adjoins the Center to the rear of St. David University. Nikki's office at the University is located in Hayes Hall, an ivy-covered brick building, just behind the Medical Center. The familiar musty smell greets her, as she enters the back door and makes her way down the dimly lit hallway to the faculty mailboxes.

Shuffling through the various end-of-year notices, she stops at a postcard. The front is a photo of two white swans swimming side by side on deep blue water. Surrounding the swans is an overlaid heart of pink baby roses. Across the top is printed, "Spring-a time for love".

She doesn't have to turn the card over to know who it's from, Barrett, her old tutorial student. Trang's youngest daughter has a crush on Nikki; maybe even more than a crush. She never forgets a holiday, and if there's no holiday, she commemorates the passing of seasons, lunar movements, and birthdays of high-ranking politicians.

Nikki admits to herself that she's fond of Barrett, even flattered by the attention. But once she learned who Barrett's mother was, well even before that, when she fell in love with Ginni, she tried desperately to dissuade Barrett from her romantic feelings and keep their relationship a friendship.

And a friendship it is, for the most part. However, the periodic postcards and their occasional accidental meetings, tell her Barrett's crush is still alive. Even Trang made a reference to Barrett still loving her. Nikki keeps the card separate from the other notes and makes her way to her office. She opens the lower left desk drawer, where she keeps a spare clerical shirt in case of an emergency at the Medical Center, and places the postcard with a stack of others that are there.

Closing the drawer, her mind is drawn back to Celine. How different the two sisters seem. Granted, they are half-sisters. Celine's father is some unknown African-American soldier who bought Trang for an hour, and Barrett's father is Douglas Fairburn, CEO of Fairburn Enterprises and one of the recently named, "Millionaires of Western New York"

He met Trang when she bribed passage for herself and Celine to Malaysia. He was already a successful businessman, but meeting his Vietnam War obligation in the Foreign Service there. Celine was only a baby then. She was only three when they came to America, and Barrett was born four years later.

Nikki plays the two messages on her answering machine. One is from a student requesting his grade, which by now is already in the mail. Another is from her old Army buddy, Max, who is now a sergeant with the Sheridan Police Department. He wants to get together for lunch, or as he puts it, "Stop over for some lasagna. Rosa and the boys would love to see ya." Nikki makes a mental note to call him and set time aside for a long visit.

She momentarily considers calling Max for advice on how to approach the Celine situation, but she already knows how he'll respond. Like Ginni, he'll tell her to stay out of it.

"Too dangerous. Too damn dangerous." She can hear him now, but she can't stay out of it. Trang asked her, and she has to try and help. Maybe it's a good thing Magpie did volunteer. There's no one else she can think of to turn to for help right now.

She heads back to the Medical Center. Ginni is in the empty waiting area writing notes in a patient's chart. Nikki sits next to her.

"She's getting some x-rays," Ginni says, looking up at Nikki. "She's pretty run down from what I can see. Blood pressure's low and a quick glucometer reading shows her blood sugar's low also." She takes a quick look around the empty room, leans in, and gives Nikki a fast kiss on the lips. "I requested a round of blood work, and I'm sending her for a CAT scan. That'll tell us yes or no. I'm a little worried."

Nikki reaches over and takes Ginni's hand. "Now Doctor Clayton, I do admire your lack of objectivity when you're dealing with people you love, but I think we have to keep positive thoughts flowing here, at least until all the tests are in."

"Thank you, Chaplain. I needed that—been working with my AIDS brothers a little too long." Ginni smiles and continues, "We may need to think of taking a vacation one of these days."

Nikki is about to voice agreement, when Magpie enters the waiting area, trying to button her blouse cuffs while holding a stack of lab/test orders. "Bloody hell! Now I know why I don't go to doctors. They just poke and pinch and try to find something wrong."

Ginni quickly gets up and helps with the buttons. "You just have to go to Mercy Hospital for one morning. All of those tests in your hand can be done then."

Nikki joins them, as Ginni says, "By the way, you two, dinner is out for me tonight. I just got called in on a consultation at Mercy. It's probably going to take most of the evening." She turns to Nikki. "It's with Anna Muscato, and I think she wants to stop for coffee afterwards and fill me in on how the sale of her practice is going."

Ginni turns back to Magpie, "I hope you're not disappointed. I'm sure Nikki will whip up something delicious. She's a great cook, and she can entertain you with some war stories, or you can entertain her."

She winks at Nikki, who just smiles back thinking all the while. *What a break! She won't be home before twelve if I know Anna. I'll have time to get to Fort Erie and the club and be back before her. She'll never know we went.*

"I'm sure Nikki and I can find things to do," Magpie says, thinking on the same wavelength as Nikki. "Take all the time you need and don't worry about us. It'll do us two mates good to have time alone to bond."

Nikki throws her a *you're laying it on a bit thick* look. Then she gives Ginni a long hug, saying,. "Goodbye. See you later. Drive careful."

Ginni hugs back. "Bye, and you drive careful too. And watch out for your precious cargo."

Then Ginni hugs Magpie, holding her for an extra moment. "And you, my dear, are the precious cargo."

"You're embarrassing me Ginni. I love every minute of it—but it's embarrassing. See you later." Magpie gushes as she breaks the embrace and joins Nikki. They walk out of the Center to Nikki's car.

CHAPTER 6

D usk comes later and later during springtime in Buffalo, but it's already dark by the time Nikki and Magpie cross the Peace Bridge to Canada. A quick right after customs, and they're on Niagara Boulevard. They follow it for a few miles and reach the downtown area of Fort Erie. A sharp left on Erie Street takes them directly in front of The Sin Club.

The Sin Club, billed as a restaurant and lounge, takes up the whole last block of the street and looks like an old converted rooming house. Two large picture windows on either side of the front entrance appear to be painted black. No lights or activity are visible through them. White Christmas tree lights outline the front facade of the building, and a flashing billboard declares, "LIVE GIRLS-TABLE DANCING-FLOOR SHOWS-PRIVATE ENTERTAINMENT".

Nikki pulls into an empty parking spot just right of the main entrance. She turns off the car and sits back. Neither Magpie nor she has said anything since they arrived in Canada. Magpie takes a box of Player's cigarettes out of her jacket pocket and quietly says, "Now what, mate?"

Nikki gives her a disapproving glare. "Do you smoke?"

"Not often...maybe when I go out...which isn't often..." Magpie stammers. "And never in front of doctor friends."

Nikki looks back at the Club entrance and says, "I guess everyone has some secrets."

"Are we going in?" Magpie takes out a cigarette and puts it in her mouth.

"Yeah." Nikki says hesitantly. "This is the only way I can think of to talk to her. Let's go."

They both get out of the car. Magpie pauses to light her cigarette, and they walk up to the entrance door. Nikki jerks it open, and they walk into the darkness. Magpie reaches for the second set of doors, but they are abruptly opened from the inside. The two women are confronted by a huge hulk of a man; nearly six foot- nine inches tall, weighing about two hundred and ninety pounds, with no neck. He appears to have a small head resting on mammoth shoulders.

He wears the largest zebra stretch pants Nikki's ever seen. They look larger than the tent she slept in during NAM. He also wears a sleeveless tank top and hordes of curly dark hair cover his chest and underarms.

Magpie's seen exotic animals at the Toronto Zoo with less body hair than this man.

"You two gurls lost!" He booms in their faces. "Ladies night is Tuesday!" Then his beady little black eyes light up, and he laughingly roars. "Or maybe you're here for an audition." He gives Magpie a small poke in the belly. "Sorry shorty! You're too flat!"

He turns to Nikki and gently pokes at the white streak of hair over her forehead with his sausage-sized finger, as he bellows, "And you're too old!" He laughs loudly at his own jokes.

Magpie's anger at having her small stature pointed out gives her the courage to say, "We've come to see the live girls, so if there's a charge what is it?" She sticks out her rather small chest and continues, "And if there's no charge—back off dickhead!" She ends with a long drag on her cigarette.

Nikki is too shocked to move or speak. All she can do is pat the white streak he touched, as if trying to make sure it's still there.

The bouncer now stands as tall as he can, crosses his arms in front of his chest and nearly knocks Magpie over with his stomach. "Oh I shoulda guessed—you're not dancers, you're dykes. You queers make me sick. You desperate to see some ass. You make me vomit."

His obvious homophobia brings Nikki around, giving her some of the false courage she witnesses in Magpie. She steps forward and growls, "That's right! We've come for the live girls and private entertainment. Now is there a charge or are you going to play door all night."

He gives them both a last standoff stare and then steps to the side, so they can enter the lounge. As they both pass him, he mumbles, "I'll be watching you two queers. Remember dat."

Nikki and Magpie take only a few steps before they are forced to stop and let their eyes adjust to the dark room and their ears adjust to a pounding sound system. A circular wooden bar starts where they enter and seems to wrap around into infinity. Every fancy leather bar seat is occupied by men of all ages, sizes and shapes. They're drinking and alternating laughing and yelling. Behind the bar, which seems to form an almost complete circle by the exit doors, is a huge, rotating, brightly lit stage. Three girls are lined up across the center of the stage.

The girl to Nikki's far left is topless and wears only a black G-string. She stands expressionless, thrusting her hips back and forth not quite in time with the music. The one to the far right, closest to Nikki, who is still adjusting her eyes, also wears only a black G-string. She is simulating masturbation with a tall silver pole that connects from the stage floor to the ceiling of the room. With every third beat of the music, she rubs the pole and groans slightly.

As the bar rotates a second time, all of Nikki's attention is drawn to the middle girl. Her black skin is shiny with sweat as she prances back and forth, attempting to dance an obviously practiced routine. She's Celine. There's no doubt in Nikki's mind. She seems much thinner than Nikki remembers from Barrett's dinner party, but Celine's five-foot-eight frame is still accentuated by her small hips and large breasts. Her black curly hair is short-cropped, and she looks very much like an African-American except for her noticeably oriental, almond-shaped eyes.

Celine wears a white G-string and white pasties with short silver dangles on them. The white glimmers off the lights and contrasts sharply to her black skin. Just as the bar rotates out of sight again, Nikki thinks she sees Celine make a quick turn and almost lose her footing. As she points out Celine to Magpie, groans from the men at the bar and from the tables in the back of the room confirm that Celine tripped.

"I think we should get a table," Magpie says loud enough for Nikki to hear over the blaring music. She points to the small round tables that fill up the rest of the room.

They walk through the sparsely occupied forest of tables and sit at one near the back wall. Just as Nikki looks up, she sees Celine again, dancing as the stage goes around. Suddenly thinking of Trang, a lump forms in her throat. An overwhelming sadness seems to cover her being, like a heavy blanket that's difficult to shake off. *What happened to this girl?* She thinks to herself. *Was this what Trang's struggle to escape...to get to America...was all about?*

A bikini-clad waitress shakes Nikki out of her dismal thoughts. The bleached-blonde, twenty-year-old wears more skin than bikini and is complete with high-heels and chewing gum. She lights the candle in the cut-glass holder on their table and asks, "What'll it be gents?" She takes a second look and quickly corrects herself, "I mean...gals. What ya drinkin?"

Nikki seems to be mesmerized by all the sights and sounds, so Magpie takes over. "We'll have two Canadian

Clubs, straight up, and two drafts—anything but lite."

"That'll be thirty dollars Canadian, cash or charge?" The waitress announces as she opens a leather receipt book on her tray.

Nikki mumbles, "Thirty...?" and her eyes seem to bulge out momentarily.

Magpie again takes control, getting a charge card out of her wallet and handing it to the girl, who disappears into the dark with the card and her tray. "I hope you brought some money or a credit card," she says to Nikki, pulling her back to reality. "Mine's nearly maxed, and we don't want to come up overdrawn in here."

"This place is so expensive," Nikki says, shaking her head in disbelief. "I can't believe this joint costs so much."

Magpie leans in close, so she doesn't have to keep screaming. "The bar tab is nothing—what do you think it will cost to get to see Celine?"

Nikki didn't think about needing bribe money. As she starts to answer in a loud voice, the music stops, and so does she. The dancers are taking a break. The stage lights dim and faint ceiling lights come on in the lounge area. "I brought about fifty dollars cash, and I do have a card. I'll pay you back for the drinks when we get home."

"Forget about the drinks," Magpie says, taking out another cigarette. "I think you can slip the waitress something, and she'll arrange a meeting with Celine. Maybe direct us to her dressing room or something." Then she moves in closer again and lowers her voice. "Your friend's daughter looks rather high on something. I'm not sure it's safe to see her alone."

Nikki nods her head in agreement. The young waitress returns to their table and plops down the four glasses, managing to spill a little out of each as she does. Then she asks Magpie to sign the credit card receipt and hands her back the card.

As Magpie puts her card away, Nikki gets the girl's attention. "Listen...," she hesitates. "I'd like to see one of the dancers."

"I'm sorry. The dancers are not available for conversation," she says rather unconvincingly.

Nikki fishes in her pocket for a twenty and hands it surreptitiously to the girl. "Are you sure there's no way I can get to see her?"

The girl slowly folds the bill into small pieces and stuffs it in the tiny bikini bra. "There's one way—but it'll cost ya."

Nikki tries to be cool. "How much?"

"Fifty cash. And that's only if she's up for a lap dance." The girl starts to pick up her tray.

Nikki starts to panic. She just gave the waitress twenty from the fifty total she brought. *What a time to mess things up. Why didn't I think of the money?*

"Here Leftenant, let me put in my share." Magpie hands Nikki another twenty from across the table.

"They only do one at a time," the waitress quickly interjects. "None of that group stuff allowed here."

"Okay...okay." Magpie gestures with her cigarette. "You go ahead. I'll watch the drinks."

Satisfied with the arrangements and with the fifty in her hand, the waitress asks, "Which one did you say you want?"

"The black girl, the one in the middle. I'd like to see her," Nikki quickly answers.

"She may not be available, and we don't do refunds. So better have a second choice ready." The waitress is all business, as she puts the money on the tray. "I'll check it out and send someone over for ya."

Nikki's throat is so dry with anxiety, she sips some of the bitter beer. "What if she won't see me?" she finally asks Magpie.

"Just play along with it," Magpie answers. "If we can't get to see her tonight, we cut our losses and come back again. Oh my God," she starts to laugh. "Look who the escort is!"

Nikki looks over to where the waitress disappeared just in time to see the neck less bouncer heading her way. "You musta spread some cash around dyke to get this one. You're just lucky it's a slow night. Come on!"

Nikki nervously gets up to follow him. She leans over and whispers to Magpie, "If I'm not back in twenty minutes, come and get me." She thinks a minute and adds, "And don't drink everything on the table."

Magpie just grins. Then she reaches over and takes a tug on the bouncer's undershirt. "Hey big boy! When you finish your escort duties, why not come back and help me with these drinks."

He looks down at her, gently pushes her hand away and booms, "I might just do that dyke! I never get the tips, ya know."

CHAPTER 7

M r no-neck leads Nikki through an almost invisible door located on the dark, side wall. The hallway they enter is also dark, except for three bright red exit signs located at various other doorways. They stop about a fourth of the way down the hall, and he motions to the door, "Go ahead. She's in there."

He heads back the way he came, and Nikki slowly opens the door. Inside is a brightly lit, gray-carpeted bedroom. All four walls and the ceiling are mirrored. A king-size bed takes up the right side of the room, a small bar is located at the back, and what appears to be a cushioned kitchen chair is to the left. One of the mirror panels opens, and Celine enters the room. She wears a flimsy, see-through, shorty night jacket, and she carries a small hand towel.

"Now don't be shy," she says, slowly slurring the upbeat phrases. "Close the door and come sit down. I don't bite, unless you want me to." Flipping on a wall switch, she fills the room with a softer version of the music she danced to in the lounge. Colored lights come on around the baseboard of the room and flash intermittently on the surrounding mirrors.

Nikki knows Celine doesn't recognize her. They only met once at Barrett's dinner party, and the drug use is more obvious up close than it was from the stage. Her eyes are glassy and her steps unsteady. The hand she leads Nikki with is cold and clammy. They're close enough now, so Nikki can smell her stale perspiration and bad breath—an addict's telltale signs of lack of interest.

Celine sits Nikki in the chair and places the thin towel on Nikki's lap. Her legs straddle either side of Nikki, as she sits on the towel. Slowly, she unties the sash on the transparent jacket, and lets it fall to the ground. Her hands go around Nikki's neck...her eyes close...and she starts to move her hips and buttocks to the beat of the music.

She dances in her own drug-trance, until Nikki gets her attention by saying, "Celine?"

She opens her eyes and tries to clear her clouded vision. Her blank expression doesn't change, nor do the rhythmic hip movements. She lets out a little laugh and mumbles, "Reverend Barnes. I am a little surprised to see you here."

Realization sets in, but her tone and expression don't change. "My mother sent you—don't say anything." She's breathing on Nikki's neck, whispering in a nervous, almost fearful voice. "They're videotaping and watching us. I think there's a microphone too."

Nikki's not sure what to do. Celine moves her body closer to Nikki's with each pronounced thrust. Nikki wraps her arms around Celine's waist and whispers back, "Your mother is worried. She wants you to come home."

Celine arches her back and moves her crotch even closer to Nikkie's, rubbing more of her body over Nikki's thighs. Nikki feels Celine's breasts rubbing against her own through the thin t-shirt she's wearing. Celine's face rubs against Nikki's neck, then up to her cheek, up through her hair. Now both of them are breathing in unison to the beat of the music.

Celine arches again. Nikki feels Celine's hot wetness seeping through to her jeans. Nikki is getting more and more aroused.

Celine keeps the beat with each slide up Nikki's

thighs, dragging her breasts back down Nikki's chest. She pauses only briefly at Nikki's neck to whisper, "I can't go home anymore, but I want out of here. Meet me at the Lord Charles Motel on Garrison Road at two o'clock, after we close."

The music is building to some kind of ending, as Celine drifts away into her own world again—a world of heat and beat and thrashing to a climax. Her thrusting gets more intense. Her breasts now caress Nikki's face with quick wet slides. They are crotch to crotch, with Celine burrowing in further and further. Nikki has tightened her grasp and hangs on like a bronco rider.

The music crescendos and so does Celine, arching, moaning and finally screaming. Her full weight pushing against Nikki's hold. Her sexual energy exploding from her taunt body in hard, pointed nipples and tightened buttock muscles.

Nikki is caught up in the orgasm. She tries to tell herself it's only a performance, a well-practiced performance, but her body doesn't believe her. Her hips start to move in familiar small thrusts. As Celine erupts in ecstasy, tiny shivers travel down Nikki's body ending in her own hot damp pants.

The music ends and Celine slowly and silently gets off, puts on her jacket, and disappears into the mirrored doorway. Nikki sits for a moment, not moving, catching her breath. Then she hastily gets up and leaves, almost running back down the hall.

Magpie is holding court again. A beer in one hand, a cigarette in the other, and Mr. no-neck laughing by her side like they're old buddies. She managed to attract a few other fellows as well, all sitting around the little table laughing. Nikki approaches the table and catches part of Magpie's conversation.

"So I say to the girls, now don't fight, there's enough of me for all of you—as long as you don't eat too much." The tiny Magpie laughs heartily and so does the rest of the table.

"Come on, we're going now.' Nikki has her by the arm and is dragging her out of her chair and toward the door.

"Sorry boys, got to run." Magpie is waving goodbye.

Mr. no-neck stands and shouts, "You'll be back next week, right Magpie?"

"Sure, sure. I'll be here Myron!" Magpie shouts, as Nikki pushes her through the door.

They get back into the car, and Nikki starts the engine. Turning to Magpie, she asks incredulously, "His name is Myron?" She shakes her head, and they drive away.

❋

With four hours to kill before she meets Celine, and the possibility that Ginni will get home before them, and worry about where they are, Nikki drives the protesting Magpie back to Sheridan. They're only a short distance from the townhouse when Magpie pleads with Nikki by saying, "But I want to help, Nikki...I feel as if my whole life has been empty for years. Here's something that finally let's me know I'm alive again. I finally feel the rush again, you know, that sort of excitement that gets your adrenaline pumping, and you know you're alive. I want to go back with you to meet Celine. I know I could be some help."

Nikki's steadfast, as she says, "I remember the war-rush too, but I stopped looking for it many years ago. You can help me more by telling Ginni what's going on and by convincing her that I'm doing what I have to."

"You know, for a few minutes tonight, in that lounge, I felt like I did when I was over in the Falklands." Magpie wipes fog from the car's side window.

"I don't like to talk about the war," Nikki says quietly. "It opens up a lot of old wounds for me. Remembering the war is too painful for me."

Magpie looks at her. "I need to talk about it. I need to let the war ooze out like pus in an infection." She looks back out the streaky window and goes on. "I realized during one of the first invasions at Port San Carlos that if I talked to someone about the insanity going on around me, the pain and the fear lessened."

"I can still hear the terrible sounds of that day," Magpie goes on. "Royal Marine commandos and troopers from the Parachute Regiment stormed ashore first. We followed the infantry, but all of us were caught in the waves of air attacks that followed. I tried to take photos of the hand to hand skirmishes, but my hands were shaking so bad, I messed up most of them. They took Argentine prisoners; most of them were wounded...just in their teens...afraid to surrender because they might get shot by their own commanders."

"It wasn't just the fighting," Nikki says in a low voice. "I can still remember the rain and the oppressive heat...skin rashes and insect bites—getting a lung full of herbicides when they decided to defoliate a piece of jungle."

Magpie shakes her head in assent, still looking out the window. "I finished my assignment about the middle of June, but the Associated Press asked me to stay a little longer. June is the middle of winter down there, and I saw hundreds of soldiers suffering from frostbite and even hypothermia. The lads weren't prepared for those harsh conditions. Neither was I. I mean, the reporters told me to dress warmly and prepare for the worst, but no one could have prepared me for the blood and the mud, and the unbearable cold. I almost lost these two fingers to frostbite."

She rubs the first two fingers on her right hand, then continues, "We spent a few days with the Scottish Troops in a sheep barn up by Goose Green. The place was full of mites and ticks, but those lads could ignore the discomfort and the fear. They would entertain each other with stories. That's where I got it from. Talking took away my fear too, and it helped me push the physical and emotional pain away."

She looks again at Nikki, who still keeps her eyes on the road ahead. "I kept talking straight through to July 12, when we hitched a ride on the Bridgeport which was going home. Some of the injured Welsh Guards were aboard. They lost so many of their unit, and many of those aboard were seriously injured. I started talking to some of them and never stopped until we reached England."

Magpie stops talking as tears well up in her eyes. She starts to sob, burying her face in her hands. Nikki, nearly home, quickly pulls into her driveway and parks the car. Reaching over, she cuddles the small woman in her arms. Magpie buries her head into Nikki's shoulder and keeps crying until her throat is dry and her energy spent.

"It's okay." Nikki brushes Magpie's back hair off her face and puts her own cheek next to Magpie's, trying to console her. "You're okay now. Just let it all out. I'm holding you and everything is okay."

"It's not either." Magpie hunts in her jean's pocket for a tissue. Finding one, she stays close to Nikki, but blows her nose and wipes her eyes. "It's not really okay yet. I think I'm going to die. My life's been pretty empty since the Falklands. Then Geneva, who did love me, dies. And now I think I'm going too, and I'm frightened." She starts to sob softly again and snuggles back into Nikki's shoulder.

Nikki strokes her hair and says, "Hey! We don't make it out of hell for no reason."

Magpie stops crying and looks up at her. "What do you mean?"

"I mean...look at your show at the Albright-Knox Art Gallery. You must be good. That's a pretty prestigious place. Maybe your flowers could never have been painted if you didn't go to the Falklands."

Nikki kisses Magpie tenderly on the forehead. "And let's not think about dying. You have Ginni on the case. She's the best. And I need you to help me hide Celine. I plan to bring her back over the border tonight. I'll call as soon as we get to the American side and are on our way here."

Magpie composes herself, wipes her nose again, and is about to get out of the car. "All right, Leftenant. I'll run interference with Ginni, the high command, and I'll scout for a safe house." She gives Nikki a half-grin. "Thanks for letting me be a part of this." She closes the door and turns to walk into the house.

Nikki reaches across the front seat and opens the door Magpie just closed. "Oh Magpie!"

She turns around and comes back toward the car. "Yeah, Nikki?"

"You can talk about the war or anything any time you want." Nikki says, still stretched across the front seat.

Magpie pats Nikki's arm and says, "Thanks." Then she heads for the house.

�

Nikki leaves again for Fort Erie. The ride from Sheridan to Canada is almost an hour each way, so more than half her waiting time has already been used up. Once over the border, she finds a small all-night restaurant near the motel and orders coffee and a sandwich. Her nervousness is apparent when she adds a piece of chocolate pie to her late night snack.

Nikki wants to call Trang and tell her what's going on, but decides to wait. In Celine's present state, anything can happen. Addicts are very unpredictable, and Nikki doesn't delude herself that Celine is any different from the rest. She may not show, or maybe her boss will stop her. Celine says she wants out, but also says she can't go home. She just didn't say why.

Nikki decides the call to Trang can wait until she

knows definitely where Celine is going. It's ten to two, and she drives the block to the Lord Charles Motel. A broken "Vacancy" sign is partially lit as she climbs the steps on the walkway leading to the inexpensive motel's registration desk.

A seventyish-looking man with thick glasses and a small lit cigar dangling from the corner of his mouth is behind the desk. Nikki walks up confidently and asks, "Can you tell me what room Celine Fairburn is in?"

The thick glasses move over Nikki like an x-ray machine, slowly from head to feet. The registration book is then turned around. All movements are in slow motion. Each page turns at a snail's pace, as he meticulously and hesitantly reads each entry. He finally stops at almost the last one and looks up. "We only have a Celine Stardust, no Fairburn."

"That must be her," Nikki says. "Maybe she changed her name. What's the room?"

After another long minute, Nikki leaves the reception area and walks to the rear of the long, one-story building. Room 64 is easier to access from the rear entranceway rather than the maze of long halls. Celine's room is the third from the exit door. Nikki knocks loudly on the door. No one answers. She repeats the knocking four more times. Nikki looks at her watch, almost two-thirty. She tries the door knob, slowly turning it. The door opens.

A shiver runs down the back of Nikki's neck, as she pushes the door open into the dark room. The air conditioner is humming loudly, and she immediately feels the cold. A warning knot forms in her stomach, as she inches her way further into the room. She reaches for the light switch, and in as normal a voice as she can find says, "Celine? Celine, are you here?"

There's no reply, and as the light comes up in the room, Nikki sees why. Sprawled across the bed spread eagle in tight jeans and a short, low-cut top, staring motionless at the ceiling, is Celine. A tightly rolled twenty dollar bill, a razor, and an unused line of what looks like cocaine are on the dresser next to the bed.

Nikki walks over to the bed. No need to hurry, she's familiar with death, having seen it too many times in the hospice and in Vietnam. She reaches down and feels for a pulse on Celine's neck. There isn't any. She moves her hand up to Celine's face and touches her. "Oh Celine! Why this? Why did this happen to you?"

Moving away from Celine, Nikki reaches for her wallet in the breast pocket of her blazer. She pulls out the photo tucked away for years in her wallet and looks at the picture of Trang and the baby Celine. The memory of how she felt when they left for Malaysia returns. The uncertainty mixed with hope that they would escape...the hope finally dies. She looks from the photo to the bed and tears start to fill her grey eyes and trickle down her cheeks.

Putting the photo away again, she wipes her tears with a tissue from her pocket. Celine was right, she will never go home again. Now Nikki needs to know what to do. Her Army training clicks in. Knowing an overdose is always investigated by the police, she takes more tissues out of her pocket and wraps them around the telephone receiver, trying not to smudge any fingerprints or to leave any. Next, she pushes Max's number.

Max Mullen is one of Nikki's closest friends. They met while both were in the Army stationed in Long Binh, Vietnam. Nikki worked at the Headquarters Communication Center but volunteered as a Pastoral Care worker at the 90th EVAC hospital. Max was a Corpsman there. Their friendship began with their mutual concern for the wounded and dying soldiers and injured civilians.

En route to one of the civilian hospitals, Nikki and Max were ambushed by Viet Cong soldiers. Nikki saved Max's life by dragging him from their jeep into the underbrush. She was shot several times but managed to hold off the enemy until the Americans arrived to rescue them.

They were reunited two years ago, when Nikki moved

to Sheridan to teach at St. David University. A friend of
Nikki's was murdered, and they worked together to uncover
the murderer and solve the case. Their mutual love and
respect continues, and Nikki knows she can always trust Max
and count on his friendship. That's why she calls him now.

She listens to the phone ring for the fifth time. He
finally answers with a sleepy, "Hello."

In a shaky, nervous voice, Nikki says, "Max, I need
your help! I'm in Fort Erie, at the Lord Charles Motel on
Garrison Road. I'm with Trang's daughter, Celine, and I think
she's overdosed on cocaine. She's dead, and I'm not sure
what to do."

"Don't touch anything! Shit! Canada yet!" Max reacts
from his gut, then takes a minute to figure out the situation.
"There's a guy I met at a conference a month ago. He's a
sergeant with the Fort Erie Police. I'm gonna give him a call.
Give me the number there, and I'll let you know if I get
through to him. Then, I'll be there as soon as I can."

Nikki starts to protest. "No Max. I don't want to get
you involved. I just didn't know who to call and...."

Max cuts her off. "I'm coming over, Nikki. I'll call the
police, and then I'll be there. Just sit tight." He stops again,
letting his police experience take over. "And lock the door.
You don't know if she had friends around...and Nikki...I'm
real sorry." He hangs up.

Nikki sits on the bed next to Celine's body. She says a
prayer for her soul. The same prayer she says whenever she's
with death. Instinctively patting Celine's arm, she wishes her a
safe journey.

CHAPTER 8

Nikki paces back and forth in front of the bed now serving as a funeral bier for Celine's body. She has to call Trang and tell her Celine is never coming home again because she is dead. Using the tissues again to hold the telephone receiver, she pushes the phone number Trang gave her. Trang answers, but the connection sounds very fuzzy, almost like outside traffic noises.

"Hello." Trang answers quietly.

Nikki recognizes her voice and replies, "Hello. It's Nikki. I'm sorry Trang. I have bad news about Celine."

There's silence, except for the crackling and fuzzy noises. Then Trang says, "Yes?"

Nikki decides to just get it out. "She's dead...looks like an overdose...in a motel in Fort Erie. I'm with her, and the police are on the way."

"I'll come over. I can be there in twenty minutes." Trang's even voice doesn't betray any emotions she may be feeling.

Nikki instinctively responds, "I don't think that's a good idea. The police will want to investigate. They'll ask questions and make reports. I'm not sure you should be here.

I'll stay with her and make arrangements to send the body wherever you want."

"No." Trang is firm. "She's my child, and I need to be with her. I'm not worried about the police questions or the sacred Fairburn name. I need to bring Celine back here."

"I never thought of the publicity." Nikki tries again to dissuade her. "But you know that whole Joe Buglio thing and The Sin Club are going to come up."

"I'll be there shortly. Goodbye, Nikki." Trang hangs up.

Nikki also hangs up the phone. And almost immediately, she hears police sirens on the street in front of the motel and in the parking lot. There's a knock on the door, and she opens it to three uniformed officers and a sixty-year-old man with a thin, black mustache, black hair combed forward over an obviously receding hairline, and eyebrows so thin they look like they've been penciled in. He wears a brown, fine-striped suit, white shirt and black patterned tie. His black trench coat is open, and he holds in front of him, an open leather wallet with identification card and badge.

"I'm Sergeant Bond, Harold Bond, Fort Erie Police Department." He puts the badge in his vest pocket and enters the room. He offers his hand to Nikki. "You must be Reverend Barnes. Max called a few minutes ago."

Nikki shakes hands, as the three other men swarm over the bedroom. Plastic gloves go on quickly, brushes and plastic evidence bags come out. Sergeant Bond moves to the body. He puts on gloves, looks in Celine's mouth and nose, checks her pockets, and moves to her jean jacket which is lying over a chair in the corner. He goes through all the pockets in the jacket, finds nothing and then walks to Nikki.

"There's no identification on the body or anywhere that we can see." He takes a small notebook out of his coat pocket and a pen from his jacket pocket. "If you don't mind, I'd like to ask some questions." He motions her into the hallway, away from the activity.

He carefully turns to an empty page in the notebook

and asks, "Can you tell me who the woman is?"

Nikki leans against the wall. She suddenly seems to need some support. "Her name's Celine Fairburn, but she registered under the name, Celine Stardust."

"And you found the body?" He stops writing while she answers.

"I was supposed to meet her here at two. I knocked on the door, but she didn't answer. So, I opened it and found her...like that." Nikki's mind is racing with more explanations, but she tries to give the least amount necessary.

The Sergeant stops writing again and looks at her. "And you didn't think to call us first? You called Max Mullen instead."

Nikki never thought about the implications of being in the same room with a person who overdoses. She suddenly remembers a newspaper story about a movie star who died from an injection of heroin, and his girlfriend went to prison because she gave him the shot. Nikki is now feeling anxious about her involvement. "Celine's mother is an old friend of mine. She asked me to come over here and try and get Celine to come home."

"Just where over here, was she?" The Sergeant wants more information.

Nikki tries to clarify some points. "She was dancing at The Sin Club. Her mother knew she was using drugs and involved with Joe Buglio. The mother tried to see her but was always stopped. She thought I'd have more luck talking to Celine."

"And did you?" he asks.

"I saw her at the Club. Celine said she couldn't talk there and told me to meet her. That's why I'm here." Nikki could feel the effects of lack of sleep on top of her nervousness.

As the Sergeant finishes his notes, one of the uniformed officers comes into the hall holding a small vial containing a milky substance. He whispers something to the Sergeant and returns to the room. The Sergeant makes another note and without looking up, says, "It appears Ms. Fairburn inhaled some very pure, uncut cocaine. We can assume the quality of the drug caused a reaction that killed her."

He then looks up at Nikki. "We will have to do an autopsy. And since it isn't likely she could readily buy pure cocaine, I'm afraid we have to assume someone gave it to her for the purpose of killing her. This is now a murder investigation, Reverend Barnes. I'll have to ask you to come down to headquarters and answer some more questions."

Nikki's mind is whirling. Her thoughts fly everywhere from getting hold of Magpie and Ginni to hoping Max really is on his way. Someone taps her arm. It's Trang, standing quietly behind her. Nikki turns and spontaneously gives her a quick hug. She turns back to Bond and introduces Trang. "Sergeant, this is Celine's mother, Trang Fairburn."

"I'm Tracy Fairburn." Trang corrects Nikki, using her Americanized name and holding out her hand.

The Sergeant gives her a quick handshake, and says, "I'm very sorry Mrs. Fairburn. Are you related to the owners of Fairburn Enterprises?"

"My husband is the owner." Trang looks at the open door to the room. "Now I'd like to see my daughter and take her home."

"I'm afraid it won't be that simple, Mrs. Fairburn." The Sergeant smoothed out his thin mustache. "This is now a murder investigation. We'll need an autopsy before you can have the body." He pauses and asks questioningly, "How did you know your daughter was here and that she was dead?"

Nikki feels the heat rise to her face. "I called her. After I called Max, I called her to let her know what happened."

The Sergeant gives Nikki a scolding look, then turns to Trang. "You may see the body, but please don't touch anything. We'll need to ask you some questions, too."

Trang moves into the room. The men are still
bustling around, dusting and packaging evidence. She
squeezes past two of them and gets closer to the body. Saying
nothing and showing no emotions, she reaches over and
closes Celine's eyes. She looks once more at her deceased
daughter and then returns to the hallway.

Trang and Nikki walk out to Trang's car parked in the
back parking lot. They decide to wait for Max before they go
to the police headquarters. They sit in the car, not speaking,
for almost ten minutes. Nikki doesn't want to intrude on
Trang's grief, so she silently studies the car instead of talking.

The car is a new, black Mercedes 500 SL with a tan
leather interior. Nikki inhales the leather smell, taking note of
the stereo, computer dash, and speaker phone. As she is
finishing her survey of the car's extras, including wrap-around
stereo sound, separate side air, and matching leather cup
holders, Max arrives. He looks tired, unshaven, and rumpled,
but he's a precious sight to Nikki. She practically jumps out
of the car and hugs him, as much as she can, around his
rotund belly. He tells her to stay where she is until he talks to
Sergeant Bond.

Max returns to the car, walking out with most of the
police investigators. The police leave for headquarters, and
Trang follows in her own car. Nikki rides with Max, filling
him in on all the details she can think of from her first
meeting with Trang, to her phone call to him.

At the station, both women give statements and sign
affidavits. Trang is told she'll be called when the paperwork is
completed and the body can be transported. She is so
emotionless throughout the proceedings, Nikki worries about
her mental state. Only when the Sergeant tells them that "Mr.
Buglio and his lawyer will be in later to give a statement,"

does Trang respond.

Under her breath, she says to Nikki, "He will pay for what he did to my daughter—for stealing her dreams and her future."

Trang's silent again, as Nikki insists on driving her back to the States. Trang adamantly refuses, saying, "I need time to be alone. I need time to figure out how I will tell Barrett and my husband that Celine is dead." Nikki backs off and Trang leaves.

Max drops Nikki off at her car in the motel parking lot and follows her back to Sheridan. As they hit the New York State Thruway, the sun is shining brightly and cars filled with workers are setting off for a new day. Nikki's glad she called Ginni from the police station to explain her delay and to tell her about Celine's death. She didn't, however, tell Ginni it was now a murder investigation.

CHAPTER 9

Max assures Nikki he's keeping in touch with Sergeant Bond. He also wants to do some research on Joe Buglio and promises to connect with her later in the day, whether something turns up or not. Then he heads for home, and Nikki enters an empty townhouse. A note on the kitchen table explains that Ginni dropped Magpie off for her CAT scan, and will then continue on to the Medical Center. If possible, Nikki is to pick Magpie up, and they'll all meet at home.

Just as she sighs with exhaustion, after reading the part about picking up Magpie, the phone rings. Yawning, she answers with, "Hello."

"Nikki! I'm so glad you're home. I was really worried." Ginni's voice brings a smile to Nikki's face, but before she can say anything, Ginni continues. "If you've read the note, forget what it says. Just get some sleep. I've rearranged my appointments, and I'll pick up Mary. Anna Muscato's arranging for me to get the results of Mary's tests while I'm there. I'm going to bring her right home, and we'll all go together."

Nikki's sleepy smile is suddenly replaced with perplexion. "We'll all go where together?" she asks.

"I know you're tired, Nikki," Ginni says impatiently. "But you haven't forgotten, have you? Tonight's the opening reception for Mary's gallery show. It starts at seven and that's back in Buffalo."

Nikki totally forgot the reception. But seven is at least nine hours of sleep away. "I remember it now. I'm heading right for bed—just wake me when you get in." She's about to hang up, but Ginni stops her.

"And Nikki," Ginni is hesitant. "I know you're upset, and I'm sorry about Celine. And even though I told you Trang was trouble, I'm sorry for her...And Nikki...."

Nikki knows Ginni is seriously upset when she can't quite find the right words. "What is it? What's wrong, Ginni?" Nikki asks.

"Nikki, will you say a prayer for Mary before you go to sleep. I'm worried about the results today."

"I'm praying right now, so try not to worry. I'll see you both later." Nikki hangs up.

Entering the bedroom, she peels off her t-shirt and jeans and slips under the covers. She luxuriates in the cool sheets touching her now achy muscles. A nice hot shower sounds great, but the energy just isn't there. Sleep overtakes her but not before she says a silent prayer for Magpie, Celine, and Trang.

❦

"Nikki, wake up." Ginni says quietly, as she kisses Nikki's cheek and ear. "We just have enough time to get dressed and get to the reception."

Nikki turns her body around and gently pulls Ginni to her. She finishes waking up by kissing her passionately on the lips. They stay nose to nose for a minute.

Ginni says quietly, "I wanted to talk to you before you see Mary." Her forehead furrows. "There is a tumor. I've scheduled surgery on Friday with Jeff Manheim. He's the best. We won't know anything for sure until the biopsy."

Nikki holds her tightly and says, "I'm sorry. I was hoping it was nothing." Her Pastoral Counseling kicks in. "But we still need to stay positive, to send healing thoughts."

Ginni just shakes her head and smiles. "Right, Reverend. So don't say anything to Mary unless she wants to talk about it."

※

Ginni drives to Buffalo not trusting Nikki's tired reflexes. The long ride gives Nikki an opportunity to explain exactly what happened the preceding evening. She leaves details of the lap dance out and describes Myron so he appears smaller and less threatening. Magpie doesn't correct her. Finally, Nikki admits it's now a murder investigation.

"And you're right in the middle, aren't you, Nikki?" Ginni doesn't take her eyes off the road, but the annoyance in her voice is apparent to all.

"I didn't have a choice." Nikki tries to explain. "Trang asked me to talk to her."

"And you owe that to Trang. You think you do anyway. And now you've been caught in the room with a murdered woman. You find the body, and you're the prime suspect." She takes a deep breath and lets it out slowly.

"I don't think I'm the prime suspect." Nikki tries to convince Ginni and maybe herself. "I just happened to be the one to find her. Anyway, Max is on the case, and I need to follow this through until I know who murdered her."

Ginni shoots an angry look at her. "We've discussed this before. You promised you wouldn't get involved in police cases anymore, and you wouldn't put yourself in danger. You promised, Nikki!"

Nikki tries to reassure her. "I won't be in any danger. I'm just going to work with Sergeant Bond to make sure my name's cleared. And Max will check out the mobsters. I'll be perfectly safe." She lowers her voice. "I saw how hard Trang struggled to get Celine to America, so both of them could have a better life. This just isn't fair. I want to try and at least bring some closure to the way Celine died."

Ginni's tone softens. "I know, I know how you feel about all those babies born to American soldiers and just left there to battle the prejudices, with no future but the street. You know I feel sorry for them, too." She gives Nikki a quick look. "But I worry about you."

"Don't worry. I'm just on the sidelines this time," Nikki says reassuringly.

They drive further with no discussion. Even Magpie is quiet until they pull into the crowded art gallery parking lot. Then she taps Nikki on the shoulder. When Nikki turns to face her in the backseat, Magpie says, "So, you heard about the surgery, Leftenant? It's giving me a bit of the wobblies— but this crowd can take my mind off it. I can also be distracted from my own troubles by helping you sort out this murder. What do you say?"

Ginni and Nikki look at each other. Ginni nods, yes, and Nikki reluctantly says, "Sure, Magpie. You're already involved, and you can pick up what I miss. You've already proven yourself with Myron."

Magpie is so excited, she leans forward and slaps Nikki on the shoulder. "Good show! For a minute I thought I was going to be sent home to bed. You won't regret this, Leftenant. I've got a keen eye and a soldier's sixth sense."

❋

Several art critics and over a hundred patrons mingle around the Albright-Knox Art Gallery munching canapés and sipping white wine. Magpie is the center of attention and moves from group to group making everyone happy. Her various-sized oil paintings are all of different cut flowers set on tables or chairs, or draped on beds, sofas, porches, and lawns. Some are placed in plowed fields, on beaches, even in garbage cans.

"In my mind," she explains to a reporter, who feverishly takes notes, "these flowers personify much of the pain and suffering in the world. The person viewing the painting should be somewhat disconcerted by what he or she sees. The beauty of the various flowers is juxtaposed by the depth of expression in their various positioning. For example, the wide-petals of the flat Lilly on the porch are arms outstretched seeking love or help, and the opening daisy bud in the corn field is youth reaching out cautiously to truly begin life."

Nikki and Ginni stand back from the crowd that has gathered to hear her. Both are impressed by her talent and ability, and both are somewhat preoccupied by her forthcoming surgery. Someone behind Nikki coughs for her attention. Nikki turns and faces Barrett.

Her old tutorial student is really only twenty-one years old. She's Celine's younger half-sister. There is no resemblance, however. Barrett is five foot eleven inches tall and about one hundred and sixty pounds. Her long black hair is worn lose to her shoulders and parted on the side. Her creamy white skin and almond-shaped eyes are her only obvious physical claim to being Trang's daughter. She wears torn jeans, a batman sweatshirt, and sneakers, all of which make her look very out-of-place at this upscale reception.

"What are you doing here?" Nikki asks incredulously, backing Barrett into a less noticeable corner of the room.

"I had to find you. I didn't know who else to turn to." Barrett's voice cracks, as her body starts to shake.

"What's the matter?" Nikki's senses go on alarm. She knows Barrett has often followed her around like a love-sick puppy, but the concern in her voice this time tells Nikki this is about Celine's death. "Is it about Celine?" She reaches over and touches Barrett's arm. "I'm so sorry about her death."

Barrett puts her hand over Nikki's. "Thanks. I always

thought she'd get out of that mess somehow. I guess she was more unhappy and confused than I thought." She tightens her grip on Nikki's hand. "It's good to see you again, Nicolette."

Ginni finally realizes Nikki is gone. Looking around behind her, she spots them in the corner. She walks through the crowd, across the room to where they stand, reaches over, and all in one move removes Barrett's hand from Nikki's, and Nikki's hand from Barrett's arm.

"You don't think you're overdressed do you Barrett?" Ginni says sarcastically.

"I'm not here for the art show. I need Nicolette's help," Barrett hastily throws back at Ginni.

"Well, I'm not sure Nikki can help you right now," Ginni assertively answers. "How did you know she was here?"

Barrett stands her ground. "I called your answering service, Dr. Clayton, and said I was your daughter, home from college, and I locked myself out and needed the key. They weren't even surprised you had an older daughter."

Ginni's mouth drops open, but before she can speak, Magpie walks up and says, "Hello. Now who's this?" She holds out her hand to Barrett, saying, "I'm Mary York."

Barrett's embarrassment causes her to answer quietly, "I'm sorry for crashing your show. I really like your work. I saw it in Toronto." She turns to Nikki and hurriedly finishes. "I need your help. Please, it's my mother!"

Magpie cuts in again. "Go ahead, tell us the problem. We're all in this together."

Barrett doesn't quite understand, but expresses her urgency to Nikki. "She's got father's gun, and she's gone up to The Sin Club. I think she's going to try and kill Buglio."

Nikki doesn't stop to think. "We have to get up there."

She starts for the door, Barrett close behind. Ginni overtakes them and pulls Nikki by the arm to a stop. "Just a minute. You're not going anywhere alone, especially near that woman when she has a gun."

Magpie is next to them. "That's right! Anyway, you're going to need me to get in."

Barrett steps over to the circle and stands next to Magpie. The contrast in their height and weight is very apparent. Barrett looks down at Magpie, then up again to Ginni. "I don't care who comes, but we better hurry."

Ginni takes command. "I'm riding with Nikki. Magpie, if you think you can leave the reception, which is in your honor, you'll have to ride with Barrett. We can meet you there." She takes Nikki's arm and leads her to the door.

Magpie looks across the room at the various groups viewing her paintings and talking. Then she looks up at Barrett and says, "Right. Well I think they all look happy, and I've smoozed with all the critics, so let's go." She turns on her heels and heads for the door.

Barrett is right behind her and in two long strides, catches up to her. They get in Barrett's red Ford Ranger and follow Nikki.

CHAPTER 10

Barrett and Magpie get acquainted on the ride over to Fort Erie. Magpie is comfortable enough to tell Barrett about the tumor and the upcoming surgery, and her fear of cancer. Barrett reassures her and reminisces about her college days and tutorial sessions with Nicolette. Each finds that the one thing they most have in common is talking out their anxiety, which at the moment is pretty high.

In Nikki's car, Ginni pulls nervously at the hem of her muted plaid silk dress. "Just what are you going to do?" she finally asks.

"I'm going to find Trang and convince her that this is not the way to handle her anger." Nikki answers confidently.

"And just how will you convince her of that?" Ginni asks.

"By taking that damn gun away from her!" Nikki practically screams.

Both vehicles park outside the main entrance to The Sin Club, and all four walk into the first hallway. Myron, as if on cue, opens the door, spots Magpie and booms, "What ya got here, Magpie, a fuck'n dyke convention!" Then he lifts her off the ground and twirls her around like a rag doll.

"Look, look Myron!" Magpie tries to maintain some decorum, as he puts her back on the ground. "It's lovely to see you and all, but we're looking for someone."

Myron raises an eyebrow and squints, trying to understand the point she's making.

"What I mean...," Magpie starts again. "is we think one of our party came ahead, and I told her all about you—so naturally she wants to meet you."

Nikki jumps in. "She's a small Asian woman, dark hair, dark eyes."

"You mean da China doll!" He booms again. "I taught she said she's auditioning. She's already in back."

Nikki whispers to Magpie, "Do your stuff and keep him busy. I know my way to the back."

Magpie grabs Barrett's arm and Myron's arm and starts talking about an ale drinking contest. The trio then moves to the tables in the dark lounge. Nikki walks swiftly, with Ginni right behind her, to the door along the back wall. They make their way down the inner hall until they reach the mirrored room. The door is slightly open, and they hear voices. Nikki can just see inside the room through the opening.

Big Joe Buglio sits on the end of the over-sized bed, rubbing his hands together. He wears a short-sleeved white shirt, and at least six strands of gold chains. The shirt is open almost to his navel, and the three buttons still closed are stretched to their limit. His clean-shaven face is covered with red pock-marks that contrast with the reddish-auburn dye job on his hair. He smiles and the wide gaps in his teeth are visible, as well as one shiny gold incisor.

"You got a lot more goin for ya than your daughter did," he says, rubbing his hands together again. "Don't get me wrong," he starts rubbing his thighs now, as he goes on, " A black-Jap is quite a draw."

Nikki cringes at his last ignorant remark and moves noiselessly into the room.

She can see Trang, standing silently, only about four

feet from Buglio. She's wearing a short, black, sleeveless dress, and her right hand is inside her shoulder-strap purse.

"Ya know what her problem was," Buglio says, not knowing when to shut up. "She was always juiced up. She loved the stuff, never really came down."

Nikki sees the gun slide out of Trang's purse. And Nikki yells, "No! No Trang!" and runs across the room grabbing for the gun.

Buglio is on his feet, heading for the door in the mirrored panel. "What the hell's goin'" on here!"

Trang wrestles the gun away from Nikki, by elbowing her in the stomach and knocking the wind out of her. Nikki goes to the floor clutching her stomach, gasping for breath. Trang points the 9 MM at Buglio, as she spits out each word, "You useless piece of shit! You took everything she had, her talent, her desire, even her life. And now I'm going to take yours!"

He's still too far away from the door to open it. His forehead starts dripping sweat, as he pleads, "Look lady, she was a big girl. I didn't kill her. She killed herself. I can't help it if the girls go for me. She wasn't even a good lay."

Trang moves closer to him. Teeth clenched...gun almost to his head. "You're going to suffer. I'm going to make it hurt very bad—just like you made her hurt...like you made me hurt."

The gun is only inches from his face now. "No lady! For God's sake!" He begs her.

She hits his face with the gun, cracking open his lip. "Don't call for God! I want you to go to hell, where you belong!"

She moves the gun up slowly, aiming it at his forehead. Suddenly, Ginni is next to her, pushing her arm and the gun down. "You don't want to do this Trang." She says calmly. "He's not worth it."

Trang is surprised at the appearance of Ginni and looks at her. This is just enough distraction to let Buglio slip through the mirrored door. Nikki's on her feet and grabs

Trang. "Put that away. We have to get out of here and in a
hurry. He'll have all of his boys after us in a minute."

Trang puts the gun back into her purse, and the three
of them walk quickly out of the room. They run down the
hall, into the lounge, and Nikki whistles at Magpie. She and
Barrett drop their drinks on the table and are speedily next to
the other three, as they run out the door.

"We have to get out of here in a hurry!" Nikki yells.
"We're no longer welcome." She pushes Trang into Ginni's
car, then realizes her mistake. Holding her hand out in front
of Trang, she says, "Give me your keys...fast!"

Trang hands them to her, and Nikki screams, "Take
off Ginni! I'm right behind."

Barrett has the truck half out of the parking lot when
Nikki, from the corner of her eye, sees the Club doors open.
Buglio, with a pistol in his hand, is joined by Myron with a
club and two other gorillas. Nikki makes it to Trang's car,
just as Ginni pulls out and speeds down the street. Nikki
jumps into the Mercedes, but is slow getting the key in the
ignition and starting the car. The men head toward Nikki.
Unnoticed, Barrett deliberately revs her truck engine and
drives straight for the armed group. The men scatter as the
truck tires squeal. This buys Nikki enough time to pull out
and follow Ginni. Barrett is right behind her, honking her
horn and waving at the frustrated gorillas.

None of the cars stop until the Peace Bridge is in
sight. Ginni pulls over to the side of the road, followed by
Nikki, then Barrett. Nikki practically jumps out of her car and
runs up to Trang's door, pulling it open in a rough manner.

"Give it to me!" She demands, pulling the purse off
Trang's lap and taking the gun out. "Just what did you think
you were doing? Do you want to spend the rest of your life in
a Canadian Prison?"

Trang says nothing, just steps out of the car and walks
slowly to her Mercedes. Nikki stomps after her and leans

against the car door, keeping Trang from opening it. "I know he's a piece of garbage," she says. "But you have to promise me you won't try this again. My friend, Max is working on the case with Sergeant Bond. They'll get Buglio."

Trang just looks at her with an angry but controlled expression.

"Promise me Trang!" Nikki pleads. "Promise me you won't try this again!"

"I won't do it again," Trang says slowly, looking deep into Nikki's gleaming grey eyes. "Celine's body is coming home tomorrow. I will never cross that border again. I don't have any more energy to deal with that man." She pauses, looks down at the ground, and continues. "...I'm sorry about hitting you back there." She looks past Nikki into the almost-set sun.

"Then put this away," Nikki says, handing her the gun. "Maybe your elbow in my stomach was payback," she says, rubbing her mid-section and finally smiling.

Trang puts the gun in her purse, just as Barrett and Magpie come up to the car.

"Mom! I hope you're not mad that I went and got Nicolette," Barrett says, as she bends down and engulfs the slight woman in a bear hug. "I was worried that something would happen to you."

Barrett releases her mother, but Trang keeps a hold on her daughter's shirt-sleeves. Barrett continues, "I need you Mom. I've lost Celine, and I couldn't stand it if I lost you too." She gives her mother another crushing hug.

Trang reaches up and pats Barrett's face. "Don't worry, baby. You did the right thing. I'm not going to leave you." She gives Nikki another quick knowing look and gets into her car.

Everyone moves back to their cars. They drive toward the Peace Bridge and home. Magpie is in the back again, and Ginni drives. Magpie prattles on non-stop for most of the way to Sheridan. Much of her continuous monologue is about The Sin Club, Myron, and Barrett.

"Blimey! Can Barrett drive that truck!" Magpie goes on. "And she's quite intelligent. Did you know she's a chef? And you should have seen her handle Myron. She's a born actress...and she's so tall and beautiful."

At this remark, Ginni turns to Nikki and makes a funny, questioning face.

"...And Barrett will be at hospital for my surgery on Friday." Magpie adds, as she continues. "Which reminds me, I never asked if I'd be convalescing at your place. I think it may be too much of an imposition on our friendship."

"No, of course not." Ginni replies quickly. "I just assumed you'd come home with us for as long as you need. Jeff, your surgeon, is one of the best in the country. He has a new laser technique that's less invasive and the recovery time is minimal."

"If it all goes okay," Magpie mumbles. Then in a stronger voice adds, "Well, that's jolly nice of you two. And you don't have to worry about staying home or keeping me company. Barrett has already volunteered to come over every day."

Ginni and Nikki grimace at the same time.

CHAPTER 11

Magpie spends the few days before her surgery keeping busy with art gallery talks and formal speeches. She spends one afternoon accepting the "Woman Artist Of The Year Award" from the Progressive Art Center Gallery. Her acceptance speech is an abbreviated version of the acceptance speech she gave at the docent's luncheon the day before.

Barrett, dressed today in a conservative, dark brown, Armani suit, listens intently to Magpie. Barrett is Magpie's official escort. Sticking close to her side and dressing appropriately for each occasion.

Or as Magpie relates to Ginni and Nikki, "You should have seen the lass today; a bright red designer suit. Now who do you know that can get away with that? And it matches her truck—what a high class dyke that Barrett is."

Ginni and Nikki just nod blankly.

Later in the evening, Magpie forgets about Barrett, and the speeches, and the awards, and makes her nightly call to Carol Doyle. "I just watered the luncheon talk down a bit for the acceptance speech and everyone seemed happy," Magpie says cheerily, as she twists the phone cord around her wrist.

"I'm sure the talk was clever and funny, as usual,"

Carol comments. As she casually changes the subject, "...I just wish you had mentioned the headaches or at least hinted about a medical problem. I never would have let you go to Buffalo alone. And I certainly wouldn't have booked the James Jarrol opening up here...I want to be there with you, especially during the surgery."

"I didn't tell you on purpose," Magpie explains. "I was afraid...I didn't want anyone to know or to worry. There's a lot of money riding on that Jarrol opening in Toronto, and it's important for your agency."

"But when you called me from Buffalo...almost every night...," Carol stutters. "You should have told me something...I really should just tell the gallery I can't be present and cancel everything."

"No! Carol, please don't do that!" Magpie protests. "I'm going to be fine. Ginni's promised me. And I think I'd be more nervous if you were here...." She pauses, then says, "I'll expect you when I get out of hospital. You did promise to come down for the last reception and go sightseeing with me. I'm holding you to that."

"Okay...I won't come for the surgery," Carol reluctantly replies. "But I may get there sooner than expected. I'm wrapping this up as fast as I can. And I'm calling Ginni regularly to find out how you're doing...and, Mary...I'll be with you every second in my thoughts."

Magpie slowly says goodbye and hangs-up. A large smile creeps over her face, as she thinks of Carol Doyle. Carol is her art agent and publicist. She's the youngest daughter of a close artist friend of Aunt Geneva's. When Geneva felt it was time to encourage and promote Magpie's talent, she hired Carol.

Magpie meets weekly with Carol, usually in one of the small specialty restaurants on Yonge Street, near the gay area of Toronto. It was Carol who insisted they go out for their business meetings. She wanted to introduce Magpie to some of the gay culture she was familiar with, and she felt a need to encourage Magpie to eat a nourishing meal.

Sometimes, they go to gallery openings or art lectures. Most weeks, Carol is the only person Magpie sees, especially since her aunt's death. She often paints for nine- hour stretches; then finishes the day or night off with enough drinks to fall asleep.

Magpie didn't tell Carol about the tumor because she hoped the tumor didn't really exist. As the headaches got worse, she knew she needed to check them out. That's when she called Ginni. She deliberately let Carol book the James Jarrol showing at the Toronto Art Museum at the same time as her showing in Buffalo. She didn't want Carol to see her cry if the news was bad.

❧

Trang calls Nikki on Friday to tell her Celine's body has arrived home. She's not having a wake for Celine, just a private funeral at Acadia Cemetery. "I'd like you to be there, Nikki. Perhaps you could read from the Bible?" Trang asks quietly. "Since you are a minister, maybe you can find some words for Celine's death. Barrett would appreciate that and her father, Douglas, would be grateful too."

"And what about you?" Nikki asks. "What can I do for you?"

"There is nothing left," Trang sighs heavily. "I know you tried to help, but saving her came too late for anyone." She stops talking for a moment and in a darker voice says, "There is one thing... leave this case alone now, Nikki. Ask your friend, Max, not to get involved either. I want this heartache ended."

Nikki is surprised by her request. "I can't do that. If the reports prove that Celine was murdered, I have to find out who did it."

"I don't want you to do that!" Trang says adamantly. "I want this all to die, now."

"I'm a suspect," Nikki tries to explain. "I was the last person with her. They may think I gave her the drugs."

"I'm sorry I got you involved. I never thought it would end this way." Trang lowers her voice again. "Douglas's lawyers are going to Fort Erie to explain Celine's history of problems. I'm sure when they finish, you will be exonerated. Thank you, Nikki. I will see you at the funeral."

She hangs up, and Nikki takes a minute to try and understand just what Trang wants from her. The phone is still cradled in her lap when it rings again. Max is on the other end. "We need to ride over to Fort Erie," he explains. "Bond has some important information I think you should hear from him."

✻

Max fills the long ride to Canada with stories about his two boys and how they're getting taller than their father. He asks Nikki to tell him about her latest pastoral counseling work, which was always of interest to Max even in NAM. She finishes her brief explanation, and he finally gets to the point Nikki has waited for, a discussion of Joe Buglio.

"He's part of the Buffalo mob," Max explains. "Very tight with the construction worker's union. But he's greedy, stupid, and likes young girls. Been picked up a few times when he roughed up some girls at his drug parties. But even though they call the cops, they all change their stories when it comes time to sign warrants."

Max unwraps another chocolate hard candy while he steers with his arms. Then he goes on. "Buglio got into big trouble with the organized crime bosses when he got caught in a sting operation the Erie County Sheriff arranged. That's the one that went to trial. They had him on extortion and everything...but the feeling is someone got to the jury."

He shrugs his shoulders. "Not unheard of, ya know."

Sucking with gusto on the hard candy, he continues, "There's some close ties between the Ontario and Buffalo families," Max continues. "That's why he was sent packing to Fort Erie. The Boys thought it was a good idea to give him a strip club to play in, so he'd go home to the wife and kids at night. Ya know, stay out of trouble til things cooled down." He throws Nikki a quick look. "The Boys won't be happy about this new trouble. And Nikki...that's why I don't think he did it."

"I'm not sure, Max." Nikki thinks out loud. "He's certainly a waste of humanity, but as you often say, that doesn't make him a killer. And he must have some charm because Celine went with him freely, at least at first."

"Maybe not so freely," Max interjects. "She was pretty hooked on the cocaine the way I hear it. He's always been a good supplier."

Nikki thinks about what he says, then adds, "But I don't think he'd cross the bosses. He's really a chicken-shit at heart. You should've seen him shake when Trang had the gun on him." She immediately realizes she's said too much.

"What are you talking about?" Max asks quickly. "Where was this gun business?"

Nikki can't find a way out, so decides to go with the truth. "Trang went to his club yesterday with her husband's 9MM. We got to her just in time and ran out of there." She sees the scolding coming in Max's face but goes on. "She gave me her word never to do that again. I believe her Max. She's done with him."

"You still think she's that innocent Mama San from NAM," he says angrily. "You shoulda called me or Bond when you found out she was over there. You both could be swimming at the bottom of Lake Erie, ya know. And I'll tell ya something else, she's no angel. She's loaded with money now, and the Feds are watching some of her dealings with Vietnam. They think she may be laundering money or buying and selling something illegal through that export business she opened over there. She's no war-victim anymore."

Nikki doesn't respond, just mumbles more to herself then to him, "I think maybe she's more of a victim now. She thought she escaped all the hustle and pain. It hasn't turned out that way."

They finish the drive to the Canadian police station in silence; each remembering their own pain from NAM. Each feeling again the disappointment of returning to shattered dreams and heartbreak.

※

They enter the station and are shown to Bond's office. The Sergeant has tea brought in, and as they each sip from China cups. Bond sorts through a folder on his desk and retrieves two papers, meticulously placing them on top of the folder.

"We found some interesting information during our inquiries," he says, brushing one side of his mustache with his index finger. "Celine Fairburn's sister has been arrested for assault. She is also the only heir now to Fairburn Enterprises. Mrs. Fairburn has relinquished all interest in the company since establishing her own independent firm, Tracy Enterprises, Import/Export Consultants." He looks up at them.

Nikki feels a need to defend her old student and jumps in, saying, "Barrett's assault charges are from when she was a juvenile. She's changed a great deal since then, and I know for a fact, she loved Celine very much."

"Love has little to do with murder, Reverend Barnes," Bond replies. "What about the inheritance? Money is always a possible motive."

"I didn't know about the separate companies," Nikki says. "I always assumed Trang would get everything."

Bond shuffles another paper. "Mrs. Fairburn set up her own company after her first trip to Vietnam. Although her company is basically a financial consulting firm, she does own an export business in Ho Chi Minh City. Fairburn Enterprises has provided the financial backing for the company, but complete ownership belongs to Mrs. Fairburn." He looks up again. "During our investigation we were made aware of the fact that your federal government is somewhat suspicious of this company. They didn't elaborate, but it appears a lot of money is moving from the United States to Ho Chi Minh City officials. More than necessary for a small export business."

Nikki and Max say nothing, and Bond continues. "There's something else," he says, addressing Nikki again. "You weren't the only visitor Celine Fairburn had that night. The motel clerk and two other witnesses saw an Asian woman driving a black sporty-looking car, enter the motel parking lot around one A.M. and leave about twenty-minutes later. We also have a record of a phone call made from the motel room of the deceased around midnight to the Fairburn residence in Buffalo."

He looks at Nikki, smoothing the other side of his mustache. "This doesn't totally get you off the hook, Reverend, but it gives us someone else to question...Mrs. Fairburn."

Something triggers in Nikki's mind, something she didn't think about until now. *Trang never asked her the name of the motel Celine was in. She never asked the name, but got there a short time later. The funny background noises on her phone were street noise. She must have transferred her residence calls to her cellular phone, in case Celine tried to reach her while she was en route to the motel.*

Nikki doesn't comment...doesn't want to share this information until she talks with Trang. Perhaps there's a reasonable explanation...or at least an explanation.

Now Max speaks up. "Does that mean you're still considering Nikki a suspect?"

Bond answers matter-of-factly, "I'm afraid so. We don't have any suspects eliminated, except Joe Buglio. It seems he was home with his wife that whole evening."

Both Nikki and Max give him a "And who really believes his wife?" look.

"Normally, the wife's testimony would not be enough for us," Bond replies, reading their looks. "But Buglio supposedly wasn't feeling well, and his aunt and uncle were also over keeping him company. And his holistic therapist stopped in with his professional trainer. He even had a private massage that evening. He was quite busy for a sick man."

"Maybe too busy," Max retorts. "Maybe he lined up enough people so there would be no question about his whereabouts."

Bond sits back in his chair, "Normally, I'd agree with you. But we both know about Mr. Buglio's unfortunate recent run-in with the Buffalo police. I don't think he would want any unnecessary trouble right now. He's supposed to be behaving himself. The Family wouldn't like it, and I don't think he's that stupid."

"But he has lots of friends to do his work for him," Max adds.

"Girlfriends and dancers," Bond adds. "And please excuse any irreverence implied here, but they're a dime a dozen to Joe Buglio. He's left a trail of them for years. There's no reason to kill them. They're usually in no shape to hurt him, just like Celine Fairburn."

No one has any comments, and Bond moves his finger to another paragraph on the report. "We also learned," he begins again in his professional tone. "That Mr. Douglas Fairburn has a substance abuse problem. He has sought treatment for it since the nineteen-seventies. It supposedly started in Malaysia when he was a government liaison there. He's been in several clinics trying to be cured, but none seem to have been successful. His most recent trip to the Toronto Merrick Clinic was just two weeks ago."

Bond looks up into the surprised faces of Nikki and

Max.

"We know he has contacts with suppliers," Bond continues. "We also know he was very disappointed in his daughter, Celine, because she would not take an active part in the business. Their fighting was witnessed by several of Celine's friends. His whereabouts on the evening of the murder has not been confirmed, but he is due here with his lawyer this afternoon."

Is that what Trang meant by getting it all cleared up. Nikki wonders. *Will Douglas Fairburn have some information that exonerates everyone?*

"That's where the case stands now," Bond says. "The preliminary coroner's report shows no sign of struggle or assault. The blood work will take a few more days, but our initial testing shows the second line of cocaine was too pure for street sale but pure enough to cause death."

Nikki and Max have nothing to add to Bond's information, but promise to keep him informed of anything they might find out that would help the case. They drive back to Sheridan, each lost in his/her own thoughts. Each trying to fit the pieces together so the murderer emerges.

CHAPTER 12

Nikki wakes to a gray overcast May skies that drizzle on and off throughout the morning. *A perfect day for a funeral,* she thinks to herself, as she puts on her black slack suit and black cleric shirt. She didn't prepare a funeral talk for Celine, yet. Usually she just calls the family for some background information. But after her meeting with Sergeant Bond, she isn't sure of what to do. Maybe she'll just talk about love and hope, not what happens to these virtues when drugs get involved.

She fits her plastic clerical collar into the shirt neckband just as she is about to leave. Magpie surprises her by entering the hall and asking, "So mate, can I ride with you? Ginni's not coming."

Nikki gives her a puzzled look and says, "I didn't think you were coming either. I guess I thought with your surgery only a few days off, you might not be up for this."

"I cleared all my gallery duties for today," Magpie explains. "I want to be there with you in case something comes up that sheds some light on the murder...and I wanted to support Barrett. She's really a good lass."

Nikki's not quite sure she'd refer to Barrett as a lass,

✤

Acadia Cemetery is on the outskirts of Buffalo, close to the small town of Arcade. The surrounding hills are now a spring-like deep green, and Nikki talks about this perfect setting for Celine's rest. "Rest is needed because of Celine's early struggles escaping Vietnam, and her later struggles trying to find her true self. Celine was a talented and intelligent woman with a promising future before her...". Nikki searches for the right words. "She was loved by her family and many friends. And this is how she will be remembered, as the loving daughter of Tracy and Douglas...the loving sister of Barrett...and the struggling searcher for self and love." Nikki ends by quoting the love passage from Corinthians.

Nikki and Magpie follow the parade of black limousines back to the Fairburn home for refreshments. Trang is serving coffee and drinks. When she hands Nikki a glass of iced lemon tea, Nikki whispers, "I need to talk to you."

Trang finishes serving the other guests and nods to Nikki. They both walk down the short wood-paneled hall to the study. Nikki enters the room first, and Trang closes the door behind them, turning to face Nikki.

"You owe me an explanation," Nikki says, trying to hide her anger.

Trang moves closer and in a soft voice asks, "What do you mean?"

"I never gave you the name of the motel," Nikki clenches her jaw. "I didn't realize that I never mentioned it, until I talked with Sergeant Bond. He has witnesses who will put you at the crime scene. He has a record of the call Celine made to your cell phone."

Trang's eyes grow wider, but she calmly continues, "I didn't think anyone saw me."

"Well they did!" Nikki shoots back. "And why didn't you tell me you were there.? Why'd you lie to me?"

Trang stands her ground. "She was already dead...when I got there...she was already gone."

Two large tears roll down Trang's face, as she goes on, "Celine called me...told me she'd seen you...was going to meet you." Trang takes a silk hankie out of her suit jacket pocket and pats at the tears. "I thought she wanted to come home...but she called to say goodbye. She knew she was going to die. She killed herself, Nikki."

Trang can no longer hold back the tears. They are as unstoppable, as her sobs. Nikki quickly moves to her and holds her while she cries. Between sobs, Trang says, "I...I...couldn't believe it. I tried to shake her awake...to kiss her...my baby was gone! Oh Nikki!"

She wraps her arms around Nikki, pressing her body closer and closer. "My baby is gone...my beautiful black baby. Who never really had a chance." She buries her face in Nikki's shoulder, her body jerking with the sobs.

"The war was never over for her," Nikki says, calming down her own feelings. "Celine never knew who she really was."

Trang's crying slowly stops, but she stays in Nikki's arms. Her exhaustion and despair apparent to Nikki, who keeps her arms around her.

When Trang is finally composed and calm, Nikki speaks. "You know I'm sorry. Every soldier who left a child over there is an irresponsible son-of-a-bitch, and I don't care how young they were or how married they were." She takes a moment to temper her anger before going on, "The police think you're a possible suspect in this case. They're going to call you in for more questioning."

Trang lifts her head up but stays in Nikki's arms. "I didn't kill her...and I asked you to stay out of this investigation."

"I can't stay out of it," Nikki says, loosening her embrace. "I'm a suspect too."

"You won't be after today," Trang steps away from Nikki. "And neither will I."

Nikki lets Trang slip out of her arms, "Why? What's happening today?"

"My husband's lawyer is delivering a letter to Sergeant Bond. A letter from Celine asking Douglas to get her some uncut cocaine. He thought she wanted to cut it and sell it herself, to provide money for her habit. He refused of course, but the letter proves she was going to buy some and must have gotten it from somewhere...and afterwards decided to kill herself."

Nikki doesn't respond. She turns away from Trang and looks out the window. When she turns back to Trang, she says flatly, "I don't believe a word of that story. It's a little too convenient for everyone. Why would she say she'd meet me, if she planned to kill herself? And why wouldn't she wait until after our meeting? I don't believe she killed herself, and I don't think Bond will either."

Anger cuts through Trang's teary eyes, "Leave this alone! I'm no longer asking you, I'm warning you!"

"I can't!" Nikki shoots back. "I care too much about Celine...and about you. I'm going to find out who did this."

Trang is next to her again, almost beseeching her, "If you really care about me...if you ever cared about me...don't pursue this any more."

She touches Nikki's jacket lapel with her hand. An electrical current dashes through Nikki's body. An old feeling, never acted on in Vietnam, seeps through her psyche. She reaches down and draws Trang close to her. They share a long, deep kiss while years and countries swirl past them like life scripts being played on a memories' projector.

Trang pulls away slightly and in a hushed voice, says, "You mustn't get involved in this."

Nikki is confused and embarrassed by her own behavior. She gently disengages from the embrace. "I'm already involved, and I can't stop until I know why I should stop searching for the truth."

Trang reaches up and touches Nikki's lips. "I have to get back," she says, turning and walking to the door. She leaves the room.

Nikki stays behind, trying to figure out what is going on and especially what that kiss is all about. She feels the old attraction she felt for Trang in Vietnam. The pull and the push at the same time. The feeling of love always tinged with some pain, some hurt so deep it permeates even Trang's sexuality.

Nikki shakes her head, trying to rid her mind of the kiss and focus on Trang's attempts to put her off the case. *Could Trang have killed her own daughter?* Nikki wonders. "No!" she says the answer out loud to herself. "Trang couldn't do that, not to Celine. She's trying to hide something else."

Nikki stops what seems like a fruitless self-discussion and walks out the door to rejoin the group. Douglas Fairburn is waiting for her in the hallway outside the study. "I need to speak to you," he says in a hushed voice. The iced-tea glass in his hand clinking with his shaking.

He crosses in front of her and goes into the study. Nikki turns and follows him back in. The light from the large side window catches his gray hair, making it glimmer. His dark grey-brown eyes are glassy and puffy. *Maybe from crying,* Nikki thinks. *Maybe from something else.*

He looks much older than Nikki remembers from two years ago when she came to Barrett's dinner party to convince him to allow Barrett to attend the Culinary Institute. He was heavier then and much more confident. Now, he looks almost gaunt and stoop-shouldered.

"What is it, Mr. Fairburn?" Nikki breaks the silence and begins the discussion..

He walks behind her and closes the door. Then he turns and says, "I know all about how you helped my wife and Celine get out of Vietnam. She told me after I met you...after she realized Barrett's friend was you."

He nervously takes a sip of tea. "I want you to know...I loved Celine. I always loved her as my own. I would have given her anything. I desperately wanted her to learn the business. Barrett just didn't have the desire or the skills needed to run a business. I was about to sign all controlling interest over to Celine, but...her life started to fall apart. I still hoped...even told her...I'd wait until she was ready."

He walks over to the leather sofa and drops down heavily onto the cushions. He looks at the floor as he goes on. "I thought I could get her away from those friends she met at the bars. I thought if I could get her interested in the business, really interested, she wouldn't want...."

Nikki finishes his sentence. "She wouldn't want the drugs. It doesn't work that way though, does it?"

He looks up at her quickly, realizing she knows more than he was going to share. "No, drugs don't work that way." He pauses, trying to size up the situation. "Drugs own you. They become your business, your life. I should know—and you seem to know too. Did Trang tell you? I managed to hide it from her in Malaysia. The stuff was easy to get there, but by the time we were back here, she knew."

He stands and walks across the room, still talking. "I tried to quit. I tried doing it myself, and I went for a cure at least four times, here and in Canada. After those hospital stays, I'm okay for awhile."

"Is that why you were giving the company away? Nikki asks. "Is that why Trang started her own?"

"That wasn't my idea," he says, trying to clarify his reasons. "She was afraid I'd lose the company, but I'm perfectly capable of running a business, with or without the drugs. I wanted to please her, that's why I decided the company would go to Celine. I'm still the CEO." His voice gets more animated. "Tracy wants her own business, so she can go back and forth to Vietnam. She still has family there. And I know another reason why she wants it...which is what I wanted to talk to you about."

He steps closer and lowers his voice again. "She

wants to leave me. After all these years, she wants a divorce."
There's a pained expression on his face, "Tracy doesn't have
many friends. No really close friends. I thought maybe now
that she's back in touch with you, maybe you could talk her
out of the divorce."

Nikki is not surprised by Trang's desire for a divorce.
She always assumed it was a marriage of convenience, to
escape and get to America. Fairburn waits for her answer, so
Nikki tries to respond more like a counselor. "Maybe Celine's
death brought a finality to an already shaky relationship," she
says in a dispassionate textbook style.

"She blames me for the overdose." He hardens his
face now. "But I didn't do it. Celine asked for drugs. She
wrote a letter asking me for them, but I refused. Doesn't
Tracy realize I wouldn't put another person through what
I've gone through—especially the daughter I love!"

Nikki momentarily feels sorry for this man, but she
doesn't trust drugs either. He sounds sincere and believable,
but she still has doubts. "I don't think Trang would listen to
me anyway. We don't have that kind of relationship. I'm sorry
I can't help." She doesn't wait for a response. "I have to get
back to the gathering and say goodbye. I have to leave now."

Opening the door, she walks out of the room.
Fairburn stands alone in the empty study with his glass
shaking in his hand.

Nikki walks up to Trang, who's talking with two
business associates and an uncle of Fairburn's. Waiting for an
opening in their conversation, Nikki again gives her
condolences and says goodbye. Trang thanks her for coming,
gives her a knowing look, and returns to talking with the
other guests.

Nikki scans the other small groups in the parlor
looking for Magpie. She finally sees her enter from the
kitchen with Barrett. Both have suspicious looks and telling
grins on their faces.

Walking over to them, Nikki says, "We're going now Magpie." She extends her hand to Barrett, who gives her a quick hug instead. "I'm sorry, Barrett. If there's anything I can do, you have my number."

Barrett walks them to the car, and Nikki thinks she spends a longer-than-usual time waving goodbye and smiling at Magpie. Although she's somewhat relieved that Barrett isn't hanging on her and swooning all over her like she has for years, Nikki feels like something has just left their relationship, and a small feeling of emptiness has replaced it.

The silly grin on Magpie's face brings Nikki back to the present reality. She can't resist asking, "And just what were you two doing?"

Magpie sits up straight, then starts to giggle. "We were snogging in the kitchen. Barrett was making me an asparagus omelet. Well, just before she whisked the egg whites, we started snogging." Magpie exaggerates a deep sigh and says, "I think she's great! I mean, she's a big, beautiful woman!"

Nikki's taken aback. "You mean kissing? You were kissing in the kitchen?" Nikki's about to scold Magpie, when she realizes she was kissing too. "Oh...she is big and attractive, I guess."

"I'm sorry, mate." Magpie changes her tone to serious. "I forgot how you felt about her all these years. She told me about your infatuation, but I just figured you were over it. I'm sorry if I'm on your territory."

"My infatuation!" Nikki almost drives off the road. "She's been chasing me all these years. I'm not infatuated with her. I like her, as a person, I mean. I'm happily married in case you haven't noticed." Even Nikki thinks she's protesting too much—especially the married part. *Is she trying to remind herself of her commitment to Ginni. Are her feelings for Trang sending her guilt messages?*

Magpie concurs with, "I always thought you and Ginni were deeply in love. So, I guess you're over Barrett and won't mind if I try to get to know her better?"

Nikki snaps back, "No. I don't care at all. Getting to know each other might be good for both of you."

No one in the car is convinced that this last statement is sincere, but neither one says anything. Both climb into their own heads with Nikki frowning...and Magpie grinning ear to ear.

CHAPTER 13

G inni sits in the Mercy Hospital Surgical Waiting Room holding Nikki's hand. Her nervousness is apparent in the way she taps her foot and stares vacantly at the immunization poster on the wall. Nikki reads quietly from her Bible, which she holds with her free hand. Barrett walks back and forth in long strides, sometimes stopping by the door to peer down the empty hallway.

She strides over to Nikki and Ginni and asks, "I thought this was a simple procedure. Magpie's been in there three hours. Is something wrong?"

Ginni stops tapping her foot and looks up at Barrett. She lets go of Nikki's hand and goes into professional mode. "Some of that time was spent on prep for the surgery. And this surgery is not simple, just less invasive."

Realizing how stressed Barrett really is, Ginni pats the chair next to hers. "Why don't you sit here, Barrett. I'll try to explain what's going on." Barrett sits, and Ginni continues. "Jeff, Dr. Manheim, is going to enter Mary's skull through a small burr hole rather than doing a craniotomy, where he would have to open the skull. Then he'll perform stereotopic surgery, which basically is going in with a micro-laser, cutting out the tumor and suctioning it out. There's less damage to the tissue this way. They then cauterize the wound automatically with the laser."

Barrett stares at Ginni throughout the explanation. Then she says, "My God! They're going into her head!" She grabs Ginni's hand. "She just can't die! She won't will she? I just couldn't have anyone else die!"

Nikki closes her book and goes over to Barrett, trying to comfort her. "She's not going to die in surgery. They do this type of surgery almost every day. Right Ginni?" Barrett releases her hand from Ginni's and clamps on to Nikki's.

"This surgery is quite common," Ginni tries to explain. "We don't have to worry about the operation. Our biggest concern is that the tumor is a meningiomas. They usually arise from the meningeal membranes that cover the brain and are usually benign. The gliomas from the brain substance are the ones usually malignant." She folds her hands tightly and looks at the poster again.

"Is that the kind that killed Mary's Aunt?" Barrett asks, keeping her hold on Nikki's hand.

Ginni gives her attention back to Barrett. "Yes. That was a gliomas, but we have no reason to believe that's what Mary has..."

She's about to continue her explanation when the red-headed, Dr. Jeffery Manheim, still in his green scrubs, enters the room. He walks right over to Ginni, and she stands to greet him. Nikki pulls her hand away from Barrett, and they both stand too.

Dr. Manheim gives his old college friend a hug and says, "She's going to be fine. Everything went very well."

"That's wonderful, Jeff!" Ginni spontaneously hugs him back.

Barrett makes a fist, throws it in the air, and yells, "Yes!"

Nikki smiles, whispers, "Thank you," to the unseen healer and moves closer to Ginni.

"The tumor was a meningiomas, about one centimeter in diameter, self-contained," Jeff continues. "I've sent it for the biopsy to be sure, but from my experience it doesn't look malignant. She must have been getting a few headaches, vomiting, maybe visual disturbances. From where it was located, the expansion could cause those."

Barrett moves into his face and asks, "Can we see her now? Will she be in here long? When can I take her home?"

Jeff laughs and backs away, then answers. "You can see her as soon as she's set up in Intensive Care. That's just a precaution for today, as you know Ginni. If everything goes okay, she'll be home in seven days. Now, I've got to run. I've got another one in twenty minutes." He reaches around Barrett and gives Ginni another hug.

He leaves and Ginni practically throws herself into Nikki's arms. "That's great! Just great! Thank you, thank you for the prayers. See, I told you to bring your book, that would do the trick. And it did!" She gives Nikki a quick kiss and reaches over for the purse she left on her chair.

Barrett takes this opportunity to also throw herself into Nikki's arms and give her a long kiss. She comes up for air and says, "Isn't it wonderful? She's going to be okay!"

Nikki backs away mumbling something about how, "It is wonderful, but it wasn't the book...and maybe they should go to Intensive Care...."

Ginni, who is too happy to be miffed at Barrett's behavior, grabs Nikki's arm and leads her out. Barrett follows close behind.

❁

Only two at a time are allowed to see Magpie. Barrett insists Nikki and Ginni go first. Since visitors can only get in every ten minutes on the hour, she plans to spend the whole day in the waiting room, going in whenever she can.

Nikki and Ginni quietly enter the cubicle. Intravenous drips are in both of Magpie's arms while various other tubing is apparent flowing out from beneath the covers. An EKG machine clicks loudly, while a monitor shows lines dancing up and down. Nikki moves close and blesses Magpie by making a cross on her forehead. At Nikki's touch, Magpie opens her eyes and forces a half-smile. Then she says in a hoarse voice, "So, you're wearing your church suit, Leftenant, did you think it would get you a free lunch?"

Nikki is so relieved to hear the wise-crack, that she bends down and plants a kiss on Magpie's cheek, whispering, "Naw. I thought I'd get a free parking space."

Nikki backs away, so Ginni can get closer. Ginni kisses Magpie tenderly on the lips. "Everything went very well," she says, her voice starting to crack. Did Jeff talk to you?"

Magpie reaches up and touches Ginni's face, brushing away a stray tear that's rolling down her cheek. "He said he got it all..." Her voice is weak. "He said it didn't look malignant...and that I could resume sexual activity in two to three weeks." She giggles and coughs at the same time.

Ginni starts to sob and puts her cheek on Magpie's cheek. "I'm so relieved, Mary."

Magpie tries to touch her face again, but her IV tubes get caught on the bed. "I knew you'd be pleased about the sex, but should we tell Nikki?" She laughs again, then gets very serious and says, "Thank you both. I know...it was your love and concern...that brought me through...I don't really know...what to say... but thanks..." Her voice trails off.

Ginni pats her arm and kisses her again. "You need to rest, so we're going to go now. One of us will check in on you tomorrow...." She pauses before continuing. "And Barrett is waiting to get in to see you. I think she's planning to spend the day."

Nikki moves up to the bed again and kisses Magpie's forehead. "If I were you, soldier, I wouldn't use the sexual activity story on Barrett. She may have a calendar with her."

"You will...keep me abreast...of the case," Magpie asks. "Won't you, Leftenant?"

Nikki smiles and shakes her head. "You'll always know as much as I do."

✹

Ginni takes Nikki's arm as they walk out of the hospital, ignoring the stares they get from visitors and staff. Ginni almost has a bounce in her step until they reach Nikki's car. Then she suddenly stops, turns to Nikki, and asks, "There is no more case. Right, Nikki?"

Nikki unlocks her door as she answers, "That's what Trang says, and that's what Sergeant Bond called to tell me. Douglas Fairburn's letter from Celine points to a suicide."

Sliding in behind the wheel, Nikki leans over and unlocks Ginni's door from the inside. Ginni is commenting, as she gets into the car. "Then why do I feel like you're not convinced, like you're still involved in the case?"

"I don't know." Nikki shrugs her shoulders. "Maybe because I think someone murdered Celine. Maybe I think her father has a motive and even her mother has a possible motive."

"Nikki! You're talking about your Trang," Ginni says, surprised by the accusation.

"She's not the Trang I used to know," Nikki explains. "She's a stranger, possibly involved in illegal business. Someone who always wanted to be rich, now she is. Abused and broken by a war she didn't deserve, a war that ruined her life—and is still hurting her."

Ginni says nothing, and they drive home.

CHAPTER 14

Another overcast day greets Nikki the next morning. She says a quick and short prayer for Magpie, pours her second cup of coffee into a travel mug, and half-heartedly walks to her car. While she drives the three miles to Easton Creek Park, she sips the hot coffee and tries to ignore the erotic thoughts of Trang that keep floating into her mind. The more she tries to push them away, the more her hormones jump.

She arrives at the entrance parking area and almost jumps out of the car, hoping to leave the Trang thoughts behind. Nikki mumbles to herself, while she walks down the long dirt path leading into the park. "I'm not even teaching a class this summer, so how did I get involved with this ecology project? Why am I here leading Troop B in the St. David University 'Let's Beautify Sheridan' project?"

She pulls her baseball cap down further and zips up her VFW Post jacket. Pushing up her left sleeve, she looks at her watch and says, "7:10 A.M., so where is everyone? I'm sure I'm not the only member of Troop B"

Nikki picks up the bright orange garbage bag she dropped while looking her watch. Then she makes her way through a narrow grove of ash trees, heading for the small creek that forms the boundary for one side of the park.

She retrieves odd pieces of paper and candy wrappers as she goes and finally reaches the edge of the shallow creek.

Small, rhythmic waves fall over the eroded rocks, gurgling and splashing. The smell of the clear water starts to lift her spirits. The water has her full attention, until the crack of a twig broken by someone's step invades the solitude.

She turns around just in time to see a tall figure racing at her with a softball-sized rock in his hand. Nikki has no place to run. The creek is to her back, the figure is right in front of her. At first, she's unable to tell if it's a man or woman, but his height and large shoulders, plus the bulge in the front of his tight jeans are a dead giveaway. He wears an old torn jean jacket and heavy gray work gloves. His entire face is hidden by a green ski-mask.

He's next to her now, swinging the rock toward her head. She ducks once, averting the blow. She grabs his arm, but he's over a foot taller and easily outweighs her, too. Wrestling with his arm, she pushes up the jacket and sees a quick glimpse of his skin. But, he grabs the front of her jacket with his other hand. He's pulling her away from the rock-armed hand. She needs both her hands to break away from his hold on her jacket.

Without thinking, she instinctively kicks his shin. He bends toward the pain, and she knees his groin. He lets out a quick, deep yell and lets go of her jacket. He clutches his injured groin with his free hand but comes at her again with the rock. Nikki starts to run toward the trees. She almost reaches the path, but her foot slips on a patch of wet mud. She goes down hard on the cold, icy, ground.

He's next to her in seconds; his arm raised to strike. She rolls over quickly, and he misses again. She tries to get up but this small muddy area causes her footing to slip and slide.

He comes at her once more, swinging his arm and losing his balance in the process. Nikki tries to get up again but slides forward. The rock just barely connects with the left corner of her forehead. However, the force of his swing, coupled with the movement of her slip are enough to knock her into the creek. Momentarily dazed, she lies still in the shallow water.

Coming back to full consciousness, she looks at the water, watching her own dark red blood float off into lighter shades of pink. The muffled sound of voices and screaming tells her the missing troop has arrived. Two male students lift her out of the water and place her carefully on the grass. She's covered with four jackets, while a clean bandana is pressed to her forehead. Another student uses a cell phone to call for help. Nikki makes a mental note to get herself one of those phones. Then she closes her eyes in a prayer of Thanksgiving for her near escape and her responsible students.

❈

The ambulance takes Nikki, against her wishes, to the Memorial Medical Center. She knows Ginni is working and will find out she's there. The University health insurance is linked to the Center, so she has no choice.

"The ambulance driver told me you wanted to go to Mercy Hospital," Ginni says softly, as she pulls another stitch through Nikki's cut. "Why did you do that? You know I'm the best stitcher in Western New York. As a matter of fact, this scare will blend so well with the little one you already have, no one will be able to tell the difference."

"I was afraid you'd be mad," Nikki says sheepishly. "I was afraid you'd think this had something to do with Celine's murder, and then you'd say, 'I told you so'. I didn't want you upset."

Ginni puts down the suture thread and takes Nikki's face in her hands. "Please, don't ever run away from me. I love you, Nikki. I don't want you involved in dangerous situations, because I worry that I might lose you." She kisses Nikki just below the stitches. "If my nagging is going to push you away, I'll stop it right now."

Nikki grabs her hand. "No. Don't ever stop nagging and don't ever stop caring. I promise this will be my first choice for health care."

Ginni smiles and says, "Good...now...did this have something to do with Celine's death?"

Nikki smiles back, stands, and scoops Ginni in her arms and kisses her. Then she goes into the waiting Room to meet Max.

✂

Max waits until they are sitting in Nikki's kitchen, drinking coffee, to start asking the necessary questions. He takes out his little notebook with the pen clipped on the front and looks up at Nikki with deep concern and says, "That sure is a goose-egg ya got." He holds his pause a moment before getting down to business. "Any idea who it was?" he asks.

Nikki pushes a candy bar over to Max and answers, "I know it was a guy. He's about six foot four or five, maybe a hundred and seventy pounds. He's wearing white sneakers, worn jeans and a jean jacket to match. He had on those gray work gloves you can buy in any home improvement store...and I think he's African-American. I got a glimpse of his wrist while we were fighting, and his skin's very dark."

"Could it be a tan? Maybe from one of those tanning places?" Max asks, taking a big bite of the candy bar. "Could it be a student, maybe an ex-student who didn't like you?"

"I can't be sure," Nikki says, gingerly touching her stitches. "But I think I'd recognize something about a student. He didn't seem familiar in any way."

Max makes some notes while he chews, then asks, "How did he know you were there?"

"Anyone could call the college," Nikki explains. "The receptionist has been giving out the schedule for "Beautification Day" all week. She has a list of all the professors and where we would be. Maybe he's a student, or she thought he was."

"And the motive? Any idea why he came after you?" Max takes another bite and chews slowly with his mouth open.

Nikki rubs her tired eyes, then looks up at Max. "I don't think it was a sexual attack or anything like that." She stares at Max's notebook and says, "I think he wanted to kill me...I don't know why, but I think his sole purpose was to kill me...and he almost did."

Max swallows the rest of the candy bar in two large gulps. "Remember any disgruntled students, maybe a parishioner who flipped out?"

"No." Nikki answers. "I can't think of anyone who hates me enough to kill me. Unless they have me mixed up with someone else." She taps the table with her finger. "Remember that guy at the 90th EVAC? Everyone thought he was Sid Benchley. We declared old Sid dead four different times, before the real one walked in. Maybe this guy thought I was Sid Benchley," Nikki says, laughing lightly.

Max doesn't laugh with Nikki. He sits up straight and flips back several pages in his notebook. With a concerned look on his face, he asks, "Do you remember a guy in NAM named, Jimmy Coleman? He came in a few times too, mostly when I was working my night shift. He was always overdosing on some kind of drug, pot, heroin, LSD. He was some kind of musician"

"Sure." Nikki answers, somewhat perplexed by the question. "Jimmy was a black guy from Georgia, I think. He played the clarinet, but he was always high. I think they sent him home early. Why?"

"Just my gut, gnawing at me." Max says, looking at his notes. "While I was waiting for you at the Medical Center, I got a call from Henry. He just answered a DOA at the Bourbon Street Restaurant. One of the jazz musicians, named James Coleman, apparently overdosed on cocaine.

The cleaning woman went in early and found him in the back room. Henry said the body was still warm."

Nikki stares at Max for a minute before speaking. "Could that be the same Jimmy Coleman from NAM? And could he be the same guy who came after me this morning? And why do I think those two facts might be related? Help me out here, Max. I've got shivers moving from my toes to my head. The same feeling I got every time there was a shelling—and we don't have a bunker to hide in."

Max closes his notebook, clips on the pen, and returns it to his pocket. "I've got that same feeling...and there's something else that bothers me. How many cocaine overdoses are you and me involved with in an average month?"

"What are you saying, Max?" Nikki asks.

"I'm not sure," Max begins slowly. "But I have this feeling that Celine Fairburn's suicide and Jimmy Coleman's overdose are related. You up to riding over to the station? Maybe Henry has some answers to our questions."

Nikki changes out of her bloodied clothes and pops two more Tylenol for her headache. She's trying to believe that if the dead man is Jimmy Coleman, it's just a strange coincidence—but she hasn't believed in coincidences since NAM. And the hair standing up on the back of her neck continues to be an old wartime warning for danger ahead.

❁

Henry Ostrow's office is as plain as he is. It somehow looks small because he dwarfs it with his very tall, skinny presence. His desk is clean and tidy with several stacks of papers, each carefully placed on top of the next, pencils in a ceramic holder, and a Sheridan Police Department mug set on a napkin.

Max takes the chair closest to his partner's desk, and Nikki sits across from the two men. Max takes the folder Henry hands him. "What have you got for us, Henry?"

Henry looks at Nikki and in his slow cadence inquires, "How are you Nikki? Looks like a nasty crack. Are you feeling well enough to be here?"

"I'm fine," Nikki says appreciative of his concern. "I've just got a bad headache."

Henry turns back to Max, explaining his findings so far. "I ran James Coleman through the computer. He's had twelve arrests, covering three states. Ten for possession, two for dealing. He's always gotten out of jail time." Henry scans another report on his desk. "Was dishonorably discharged from the Army in 1968. No charges filed, probably because he spent his last eight months in Vietnam."

This gets both Nikki and Max's attention. Max points to a section of the report he's reading. "It says here, the probable cause of death is a self-inflicted drug overdose. Did you test any of the drug at the scene?"

"There was very little powder around," Henry explains. "Even his spoon was clean...which I found rather suspicious for an overdose. So I had one of the boys scrape his nose. It's pretty pure cocaine according to our kit test. I've asked the coroner to run a blood tox." He stops, sits back in his chair, and asks, "What's the story, Max?"

"I think this may be murder," Max says frankly. "And I think it's tied in with the Fairburn case in Fort Erie."

"I thought that was declared a suicide and put to bed," Henry comments.

Max shakes his head affirmative, but says, "We may have to wake it up again, if we find a tie between the two."

Nikki is almost thinking out loud when she says, "Both have links to Vietnam around the same time period. Both were addicts, and both appear to have died of drug overdoses from very pure cocaine. But what could the real link be?"

Max is all business, as he says to Henry, "See if you can find any connection between Coleman and Buglio.

I don't care how remote. Coleman got his drugs from someone. See if the mob is involved somehow." He checks the report again. "What about family? Does Coleman have relatives?"

"He has an ex-wife and two children in their twenties, back in Georgia. That's all we could get out of the musicians he plays with. He wasn't very close to them," Henry explains. "He also has a third wife in Buffalo. Don't know what happened to the second one, but he just married this one about a year ago. I sent an officer to break the news and tell her we need to talk to her."

"When do you expect to call her in?" Max asks. "I want to be in on that interview."

"I want to ask her a few questions, too." Nikki chimes in.

Both men look at her, Max says. "You can give me your list of questions, Nikki, but you can't be there. We have to be careful about her privacy." He pauses before going on, "You know I'll keep you posted on this one."

Max turns back to Henry. "Has the body been moved to the morgue yet?"

"I think it's still at Mercy Hospital," Henry says. "You know how backed up the coroner is. I think he said he'll send the wagon tomorrow morning."

Max stands abruptly. "Come on Nikki. I want you to get a look at this guy and see if you can place him at your assault."

I don't think that'll be necessary," Henry interjects. "We found this under his body. He fell on it when he went down." He opens his side desk drawer and pulls out a green ski mask, identical to the one Nikki's assailant wore.

"And here's a description of what Coleman was wearing when he died." Henry picks up another report and reads, "Worn blue jeans, a long-sleeved matching jean jacket, white sneakers." He looks up. "I think he's the one that assaulted you."

Both Max and Nikki agree. They found the man who tried to kill her, but who killed him? And why? And what is his tie to Celine Fairburn. They may know who Nikki's assailant is, but there are still more questions than answers.

CHAPTER 15

Nikki walks down the hospital corridor carrying the plastic shopping bag filled with miniature Snicker bars, Magpie's favorite food. Entering the room, she sees Magpie and Barrett locked in an embrace, fervently kissing. Barrett leans over Magpie, who is lying on the hospital bed. The only visible sign of Magpie's surgery is the four inch square bandage on her forehead.

Magpie finally eases her head back onto her pillow and opens her eyes. She sees Nikki in the doorway and gently pushes Barrett away. "Come on in, Nikki. Barrett was just saying goodbye."

Barrett turns to Nikki, tries to hide her embarrassment, and says, "Yeh...um...that's right. I got to go." She turns back to Magpie and explains, "But I'll be back tonight. I'll read some more to you."

Giving Magpie a quick kiss, she starts for the door. "Bye, Nikki. Good to see you," she says trailing off down the hall.

Nikki moves closer to the bed and hands Magpie the bag. "You look better every time I see you." She sits in the chair next to the bed.

Magpie rummages through the bag. "This is great! All my favorite things, Snickers and more Snickers!" Then she notices the stitches on Nikki's forehead. "Hey, Leftenant?

What happened to you?"

A promise is a promise, Nikki reminds herself. Then, she proceeds to tell Magpie the story of the assault, and the possible link between Jimmy Coleman and Celine Fairburn. "Max and Henry are questioning Mrs. Coleman right now," she adds.

"So now we have two murders!" Magpie says enthusiastically, munching one of the candy bars. "And you and Vietnam are the links."

"Wait a minute," Nikki jumps in. "I'm not sure about Vietnam. I mean, both Coleman and I were there, but I'm not sure that's the tie. I think the cocaine is the tie."

"Oh," Magpie says, sounding unconvinced by Nikki's explanation. After another pronounced bite, she perks up again, quickly saying, "What's our next step?"

Nikki gives her a stern look and replies, "We don't have a next step. You're going to heal, so you can get out of here. We also have the spare room waiting for your recuperation days."

"But Nikki," Magpie pleads. "I'm practically there. I'm getting released at the end of the week, and I can do a lot of research on this from your house." She pauses for emphasis. "Remember, Barrett is with me almost every day. I can always get information from her."

Nikki is somewhat taken aback. "You're not saying you're stringing her along for information, are you?"

"I'm not stringing her along." Magpie smiles. "She's being attentive to me because she still wants to be close to you. I enjoy the attention, so I go along with it. But I'm realistic. She uses me a bit, so I feel I can use her a bit."

Nikki doesn't know how to address this turn of events. "Are you sure? Barrett seems to really like you— maybe more than like."

"Maybe she thinks she does," Magpie explains. "Maybe she wants to be in love with me, but she isn't.

She sprinkles too many conversations with 'Nicolette this and Nicolette that'. I don't mind, Nikki. I haven't had anyone gushing over me in a long time, and I like it. I'm just being realistic."

Nikki decides to drop the subject, before she hears more than she feels like dealing with. Noticing a large bouquet of flowers on the night stand, she says, "The flowers are really beautiful; sort of a head start on summer. Barrett has expensive tastes."

"They are lovely," Magpie says touching a petal on one of the roses. "But they aren't from Barrett. They're from Carol Doyle, my agent. She's coming down for awhile to see me and to get the rest of the art show commitments rescheduled. You and Ginni will get to meet her."

Nikki tries to stay upbeat. "That'll be nice for you, someone from home." Moving closer to the bed, she gives Magpie a warm hug. "I've got to run...but I'll keep you posted."

She leaves the hospital thinking about the change in her opinion of Magpie. She likes her, and she hopes the relationship with Barrett is bringing her some joy. Magpie needs more joy in her life—something good enough to replace the Falklands' bad. Maybe love will still come into that relationship. But Magpie's romantic life seems minor compared to the complications surrounding this case and Jimmy Coleman. She wonders how Max's interview is going.

❁

The surface of Max's desk is a complete contrast to Henry's. Every square inch is covered with papers and reports in every size and color, pieces of waxed paper from old lunches, half-used napkins, loose pencils, Styrofoam cups, and several stacks of manila folders. He sits behind his desk, writing on a yellow legal pad. Henry is next to him, listening attentively.

Mrs. Darla Coleman sits across from them, twisting the shoulder strap of her purse nervously, as she talks.

"I told them when they called, just send the body back to his kids in Georgia." She tugs at the bottom of her mini-skirt, trying to force it closer to the knee of her crossed leg. "We were through. I tossed him out about two weeks ago. Drugs, that's all he had on his mind, day and night."

She uncrosses her leg and taps her three inch heel nervously on the floor. "He was getting too weird for me. And he never managed to get his paycheck from work to home." She leans forward, causing her loose, low-cut shell to drop even further. "I've been supporting myself for months. I didn't need him."

Henry clears his throat and slowly asks, "When you say he was getting weird, what exactly do you mean?"

She sits upright, trying to match his perfect posture. "There was this girl," she explains. "A real pretty thing, mixed, you know."

Max asks, "What do you mean, mixed?"

"I mean," she says in a bothered tone, "She wasn't all black. She was part Japanese, or Caribbean, or something. Anyway, she started hanging around. Calling him at home, meeting him at his gigs." She rubs one of her long, African-symbol earrings. "He says it's strictly business. Well, I laughed in his face and told him no God-damn hoe is gonna get my house money. He goes on and on about how this kid thinks he's her father, from sometime when he's in the Army, and..."

Max interrupts again. "He said she thought he was her father? That she was his daughter from when he was in Vietnam."

"Yeah," she points at him with her finger. "Yeah, it was that Vietnam shit. Anyway, she wants to snort with him, and I think they did. I think he blew a lot more money than he brought home. So I'm very pissed at Miss Trang, and he tells me she's really some rich guy's kid, and she's gonna take over this business, and he's gonna get rich. So, I know this is coke-shit talking and I tell him dump the kid or take a walk." She stops talking. "And that's the last I saw him, last Tuesday night. He walked, and I made plans for myself. I got guys waiting in line. He was gonna be a big musician, cut another record. He was always full of shit and now..." She shrugs her shoulders.

"Do you think you could identify this girl, if you saw her picture," Henry asks.

"I never saw her," Mrs. Coleman answers, studying her cuticles. "Jimmy told me what she looked like. I didn't want to meet his latest lay. I got better things to do."

Max makes another note and stands up. "Thank you for all your cooperation, Mrs. Coleman. We'll let you know if we find out anything."

"I don't give two shits about what you find out," she says standing and brushing off her skirt. "I only want to know if there's money involved. And as far as I'm concerned, this is my last freebie. You want any more information, and you'll have to pay."

She turns to leave. Henry takes two long steps and reaches the door before her. He opens it, and she gives him a nod as she walks through.

�֍

Max is again sitting at Nikki's kitchen table drinking hot coffee and munching cookies. Nikki sits across from him warming her hands by wrapping them around her coffee cup. Ginni is next to Nikki, listening intently while she dunks her tea bag in and out of her cup.

"I can't believe Celine would think Jimmy was her father," Nikki says to Max.

"Why not," he answers, talking while he munches the cookie. "For all we know, he coulda been. He was in NAM at the right time. Most of those guys frequented the prostitutes."

"But how would she find him?" Ginni asks.

"They have organizations now," Max explains. "They got one in Buffalo called 'Amer-Asian Father Find'. I called them up to see if Celine Fairburn contacted them. They didn't want to tell me, but I threatened a court order. They told me they gave her a list of known vets from that time period. They also advise their members to check out phone books for the most inexpensive way to find someone. Coleman must have been high on the list, and bingo she finds him in the same city."

"Why, Max?" Nikki asks. "Why would she want to find him now?"

"A child always wants to know about her real parents," Ginni answers first. "In Celine's case, she probably had a lot of questions that Trang couldn't answer...or didn't want to answer."

"It gives us a link between the two murders," Max says solemnly. "I've called Bond, and he's looking into reopening the Fairburn case. He needs some more proof though not just coincidences. And, Nikki?" Max stops and plays with the spoon in his cup. "The biggest question I have is why did he want to kill you? What did he think you knew, or know?"

Nikki looks puzzled. "I don't have any idea, Max. I've been trying to figure out why he attacked me at all. Unless he was involved in Celine's murder and saw me at the motel..."

"Or someone else is involved, someone who doesn't want you nosing around, someone calling the shots," Max continues her reasoning. "This person thinks you know too much and need to be eliminated."

Ginni suddenly spills her tea. "I don't like this at all," she says, mopping up the tea with extra napkins. "I don't like you being anyone's target. And I hate to repeat myself, but I told you Trang is trouble. That whole Fairburn family is trouble."

"But I don't know anything," Nikki says trying to reassure Ginni. "The attack had to be more of a mistaken identity thing. I can't tie anyone to anything."

Max throws her a knowing look. "Well, someone thinks you can. And I agree with Ginni. I don't like this either. So lay low for awhile. Let me and Henry do the nosing around. I'll let you know what we find."

"Okay...Okay. I don't need my head bashed in," Nikki says." I'll stick close to home and stay out of police work." She looks at Ginni and says, "Will that make you happy?"

"Yes," is Ginni's prompt reply.

❧

A day after her conversation with Max, Nikki calls Trang and insists on seeing her. "I have a few questions that need answers," she says, rubbing the stitches on her forehead. "And I want to ask you in person. I can come to your home or your office, but I need to see you today."

Trang reluctantly agrees to see her at her office. Her company has the entire sixth floor of the Fairburn Enterprises Building. She'll meet Nikki at two o'clock.

CHAPTER 16

Nikki wears her pressed jeans and a favorite paisley print, short-sleeved, purple shirt. She puts a beige linen blazer over the shirt to dress up the outfit, but forgets she's wearing white Nike sneakers. She tries to comb her hair down over the stitches, but her white streak and blonde hair seem almost transparent and the black x's and blue-yellow bruise still appear through her hair.

Fairburn Enterprises is located in an old box factory on Buffalo's waterfront. The historic building was completely remodeled into one of the most modern office buildings in the city. Leather and glass seem to be the running theme of the decor, with Jackson Pollack paintings taking over complete walls. This means that at the top of each open staircase is a wall canvas full of splattered paint, expensive modern art.

Nikki enters the main foyer and is immediately impressed with the arboretum and waterfalls located at the back of the long room. Benches surround the area with workers taking their breaks in the private botanical gardens. When she introduces herself to the guard, he checks a book and gives her a pass. He then directs her to the elevators, "Mrs. Fairburn's office is on the seventh floor."

Stepping off the elevator, Nikki enters the world of corporate chic. Plush gray carpets roll on forever. Their journey broken only by glass walls and door partitions. Computers, fax machines, copiers, and even telephones are all color coordinated in beige/gray tones. Several work cubicles are also visible, each partition the same color as the rug.

She enters through the glass doors labeled "Tracy Enterprises". A receptionist, sitting at a similar beige/gray toned desk, listens to her request to see Mrs. Fairburn and gets up to escort her down a gray lined corridor. Nikki feels underdressed as the young Vietnamese woman, wearing a black mini-suit walks ahead of her.

They stop in front of large walnut doors with "Tracy Fairburn, CEO" on them. The receptionist knocks twice, opens the door slightly, and puts her head inside. She finishes opening the door and says to Nikki, "You may go in now."

The door closes behind her, and Nikki finds herself in the biggest office she's ever seen. A large overstuffed leather sofa and chair with a matching walnut coffee table are at the end closest to the door. At the far end is an almost wall to wall walnut desk, computer, fax machine, television, small bar and refrigerator. The three remaining walls are all windows covered with beige vertical blinds. The blinds are open and the view is of the panoramic vista of Lake Erie.

Trang enters the room from one of two doors behind either side of her desk. She carries the glass pot of a cappuccino machine filled with water. "I thought you might like some coffee," she says moving to the machine at the end of a credenza matching her desk.

As she adds the beans to the machine and starts the process, Nikki moves closer to her desk. She can't help but notice that Trang is wearing her hair down. It's long and loose, the ebony color glimmering in the sunlight beaming off the lake through the windows. Trang has on a navy mini-suit skirt and two-inch matching heels. Her jacket is over her desk chair, and her white long-sleeved blouse has three top buttons unbuttoned.

Trang finishes with the machine and turns to Nikki. "Now what did you want to ask me?"

"Did you know Jimmy Coleman?" Nikki blurts out.

"Why don't we go sit where it's comfortable," Trang says, leading Nikki to the sofa and chair.

Nikki sits uncomfortably at the edge of the middle cushion of the sofa. She waits for Trang to sit in the chair across from her before repeating, "Well, did you know him?"

Trang holds Nikki's eyes with her own. "Yes. I know of him. Celine thought he was her father. She went to see him several times, and I think she did drugs with him."

"And was he her father?" Nikki shoots back, angry at something but not sure what.

"Of course not," Trang answers calmly, not releasing her stare. "I tried to explain to Celine, not because I wanted to, but because she said she had to know."

Twisting her wedding band, Trang goes on. "Celine always felt different. We took care of her material needs, but now I realize we never filled her emotional ones. She wanted to know who she really was...Celine needed a link to her past, her roots. Knowing who her real father was, she believed, would fill the void in her being."

Trang pauses, breaking eye contact with Nikki. "I tried to explain what it was like over there. My mother and father were dead. My sisters and brothers all gone, taken by the Vietnamese Army or the Viet Cong...probably dead. I had no family...no food. I don't think she could really understand that my own aunt suggested the street. There was no place for me, because they were starving also."

Trang looks past Nikki now, staring out the window, as if it is a magic mirror showing her the past. "I went to the street. There were always pimps looking for young girls, and hundreds of American soldiers just waiting for a chance to be a man. Filthy and rough, drunk, drugged, and laughing at us like we were nothing but pieces of meat they paid for."

She looks at Nikki again as she continues. "I slept with only six soldiers. I couldn't stand that kind of sex. I would cry and beg and be sick after each one. The pimp took the money and threw me out. I went back to my aunt's. Her husband was killed, and I was pregnant. So I kept house while she worked the streets. A forty-year-old mother of three, very religious, but she had to work the streets. I would take the children with me and go through the garbage cans at the back of the restaurants. Sometimes that was the only food.

My aunt came home beaten and with bruises....After Celine was born, she moved to a cousin's home in Da nang. I told her I would be okay. I would do the streets again. But I didn't like the pimp watching my baby. That's when he told me he needed a woman for a woman soldier. You were my last chance to be a successful prostitute."

Trang pauses for a moment, again making eye contact with Nikki. "Strange how that worked out. I became your Mama San instead. I didn't mind doing the laundry or cleaning your hooch. I would touch your clothes and read your books. I knew America was where I had to go. If I could get my baby to America, she would grow up safe and secure. She would never have to live like I did or have the heartbreak that I had...Too bad it didn't work out that way."

Nikki is overwhelmed with memories of the war. She can visualize the abuse Trang suffered. She lowers her voice, asking, "Was Coleman one of them?"

"No," Trang answers bitterly. "Of the six, only two were black, and I remember both their faces. I even remember their names. I could read their names on their dog tags and their shirts. I would memorize their names while they were doing me. I would tell myself that one day I would find them and make them suffer like I did."

She looks at the floor. "He wasn't her father. I tried to tell her that." A tear rolls down Trang's face, as she studies a spot on the rug.

This is too much for Nikki. She's on her feet and next to Trang. Kneeling, she takes Trang into her arms.

"I'm so sorry. I knew it was bad, but I never knew just how bad. I'm sorry for all of them and for my own behavior."

Trang puts her arms around Nikki's neck and says softly, "But you only wanted to kill me. You at least were honest enough to say your lover had been killed, and you wanted revenge. You didn't want to rape me...and you helped me, Nikki." She takes Nikki's face in her hands. "You helped Celine and me get away. You helped us to freedom. I knew how badly you felt. I knew what kind of a person you really were."

Nikki is near tears, flashbacks consume her mind and blur her feelings until they are raw and out of control. She leans in quickly and kisses Trang, long and passionately. Trang kisses back amorously, soft and searching at the same time, testing but not retreating. Nikki's engulfed in swirling emotions. They continue to kiss, mouth to mouth, tongues gliding and sliding back and forth, dancing to their own music.

Nikki is off her knees, her body pressed against Trang's on the chair, her hands move up Trang's back, fingers kneading soft skin. Trang has her arms around Nikki's waist, holding her tighter and tighter as if they are twirling together on an amusement park ride.

Trang pushes away, catching her breath, as she says, "The door, I have to lock it."

Nikki is panting, taking short, quick breaths as she backs off the chair and stands. Trang gets up and moves toward the door. Nikki's hand slowly moves down Trang's back, as she walks away from her.

Trang locks the door and comes back to Nikki. Taking her by the hand, she leads her to the sofa where she pulls a patterned throw from the back and lays it on the leather cushions. She's in Nikki's arms again, both kissing and caressing.

They try to drive out the demons of their shared history by arousal and almost-manic sexual prodding.

They're lying on the sofa now, side by side, hands searching curves and sinews. Their lips only part for short gasps of breath. Trang unbuttons Nikki's blouse, gently pulling it open. Nikki helps finish the task by slipping her blouse and jacket off together and dropping them to the floor. While they separate for this endeavor, Trang slides her arms around Nikki and unfastens her bra, tugging it off at the same time as the other clothes.

They're locked again in an embrace, Nikki moving her hand across Trang's breast to the few buttons left undone. They're quickly unbuttoned. While Nikki kisses Trang's neck from her ear down to her cleavage, she pushes off the blouse and unfastens the bra. Trang pulls the bra the rest of the way off.

Together now, skin to skin with a white-hot, electricity flowing through both bodies. Glued by passion, they are touch, feel, and raw sexuality. Rolling on top of Trang, Nikki's hips begin to move in an involuntary thrusting rhythm. Trang reaches up to unbuckle Nikki's belt, slipping her hands down Nikki's jeans as far as they can reach.

Nikki is lost in the kissing, her hand gently grabbing Trang's small breasts, brushing her fingers over the taunt nipples. They are lost in sweat and sexuality, each moving closer to finishing this foreplay. Trang is unzipping Nikki's jeans. Nikki is unbuttoning Trang's skirt. Both are breast to breast, mouth to mouth...when they hear three knocks on the outer door.

"Ms. Fairburn? Your husband is here," the young receptionist announces. "Are you available to see him?"

Nikki is still on top of Trang. Both are panting race horses cooling down after the Derby. Trang lifts herself on one elbow, finally finding her voice. She slowly and loudly answers back to the door, "Tell him I'm in a conference. I will call him later. And Vu, hold all calls until I tell you I'm free."

Silence is heard outside the door, and Nikki lies back down on Trang. They don't kiss this time. She slides to the side of the small woman, keeping her arm draped over her. Again, they lie side by side. Nikki touches Trang on the cheek, stroking her face gently.

"What do you want, Nikki?" Trang asks softly. "I will give you anything right now, but you need to realize...twenty years have passed. You took away my pain again, for a few moments, but it comes back. My pain always does." She stares at the ceiling.

The heated passion is gone, but a bond, an understanding, keeps them next to each other, flesh touching flesh. "I've always cared about you, Trang," Nikki whispers. "And I cared about the baby, even when I didn't know where you were. All your love was in Celine."

"And my hope and dreams." Trang finishes the thought.

Nikki tries to comfort her. "But look at what you built. Look at where you are now. And you have Barrett and Douglas."

"I love Barrett, of course, she is my second child." she says snuggling in closer to Nikki's chest. "There is no love left for Douglas. I tried to care for him, but he is too self-destructive. I am grateful that he married me and gave Celine a chance to see freedom, but I have nothing left for him."

Nikki touches Trang's face again, then brushes her lips across Trang's neck, just below her ear. "I'm so sorry about what happened to Celine..." She pauses, looking deeply into Trang's eyes. "I feel like I also lost something precious."

"We keep losing those we love, Nikki," Trang says. "That's why I will not love you. That's why this is the first and last time this will happen."

Nikki smiles and touches Trang's forehead with her own. "I know. This had to happen but won't happen again."

"Consider my debt paid," Trang says, smiling back. "Unfortunately, you are short-changed again. But now maybe we can bury the war, together."

They release their hold on each other, get off the sofa, and start dressing. Trang is buttoning her blouse, when Nikki says, "Why did you want me to stop trying to find the murderer? You know she was murdered, don't you?"

Trang looks at her and says, "I'm afraid you may draw attention to my business. I can't afford that right now."

"The government is already watching you. They think you're laundering money or smuggling contraband out of your export business in Vietnam," Nikki says in a concerned voice.

Trang stands still. "And what do you think?"

"I'm not sure," Nikki says. "But I think you're doing something besides exporting."

Trang smiles. "You were always too smart to be a soldier," she says seriously. "I'm paying off various politicians in Ho Chi Minh City. I'm trying to get two of my relatives over here. One of them is my uncle, the one I lived with outside Long Binh. He is in his eighties and has had tuberculosis. It costs a great deal of money to get an old, sick person into the United States.
And the second person is my sister, Tran. She didn't die. I never knew, but she found my uncle about three years ago. She fought on the side of the Viet Cong and would not be considered a desirable emigrant either."

"That's why you don't want me to pursue the murder," Nikki asks, putting it all together. "The transfer of money for people is too fragile for an investigation."

"Yes. Celine is gone...nothing will bring her back." Trang says, sighing. "And I will have revenge, but not until my relatives are safely here. So, will you stay out of it now?"

"It's too late," Nikki says sadly. "Jimmy Coleman tried to kill me, and then was found dead from an overdose of cocaine. I think Celine's case will be reopened."

"Shit!" Trang says in frustration, as she sinks down into the sofa cushion.

Nikki sits next to her and takes her hand. "Maybe I should get involved and try to find out quickly who killed them, and end this for good."

Trang moves next to Nikki, so their thighs touch. "I think this is too big for amateurs, even soldier-priests. I don't want you getting hurt. I may not want to sleep with you, but I do care about you. I think Celine was a pawn in a much larger game. My baby was the last spoil in that war."

They sit in silence for a few more minutes, until Trang gets up and walks to her desk. "I really have to get back to work. I have calls, and I need to see what Douglas wants."

"Right," Nikki echoes, tucking her shirt in her jeans. "I have to get back to Sheridan. I'll call if I find out anything."

She walks to the door and as she opens it to leave, Trang says, "Be careful, Nikki."

CHAPTER 17

Magpie struggles through the mud and bogs at the Port San Carlos's Sheep Station. Each step is an effort, like attempting to pull your foot out of quicksand. She carries her camera over her head with the strap still around her neck, trying to protect it from splashing mud. Her lined pants are coated with oatmeal thick ooze, and her hands are numb from the cold that creeps through her two pair of gloves. The thick wool scarf around her neck is wrapped twice and meets the bottom of her wool knit hat.

The Sheep Station is also the base camp of the Royal Army Medical Corps. It's a field of dug outs and huts polka-dotted with bullet and shrapnel holes. Everywhere is quiet except the whoosh of her feet being pulled out of the mud for another step. She needs to make it back to the dug out. Hard to remember when she last ate...shared some hard biscuits and coffee with the boys. No cigarettes left. Her socks are rotted through with the wet. They've been wet for days...seems like weeks... and the numbness is now a painful tingling.

Battle casualties are treated by the medics where they fall. She passes two triage teams before she reaches the dug out. A dead body lies waiting for transport...staring at all who enter. A medic welcomes her into a dry corner while he grabs a first aid bag and leaves to tend more fallen comrades.

Magpie drops down on a make-shift bunk and tries to unglue her boots; the cold mud sticks like a black honey. Next, she peels off what's left of her socks, dropping them like sponges full of water. She takes a small towel from her camera bag and slowly wipes her ankle, then her foot. As she reaches her bluish-red foot, she realizes she can't feel it anymore. She gives it another hard rub with the towel...and her foot falls right off...leaving only a bloody stump...

Magpie screams as loud and as long as she can. But her voice can hardly be heard. She cries and screams for help again. And suddenly, someone is holding her, rocking her back and forth, calmly saying, "You're all right Mary. It's only a dream...It's just a dream."

Magpie fights to open her eyes. She's on the sofa in Nikki and Ginni's living room. Ginni is holding her, rocking her, trying to bring her out of the dream. "My God! My feet!" Magpie says nervously. "I have to check my feet." She swings her legs off the sofa and tears off her socks.

Wiggling her toes back and forth, she says, "I thought I lost them. I thought they came off from the frostbite."

Ginni is next to her, putting a comforting arm around her. "You're okay. Your feet are okay too. How often do you have these war dreams?"

Magpie lets Ginni give her another hug before answering. "I still get them quite often," she tries to explain. "I can go for a few weeks, even a month stretch with no flashbacks, no dreams. Then something seems to trigger it, a song, a picture, the way some guy looks. I was watching the tellie just before I fell asleep. This big bloke was selling coffee, and he sort of reminded me of one of the Gurkhas who brought me a cup once before I fell asleep...I guess that's what set me off."

"Do you want to talk about the dream," Ginni asks. "Or the war for that matter?"

"Naw," Magpie puts her socks back on. "I'm getting a bit sick and tired of talking about war. I just want it to go away. The Falklands War has taken more of my life than any romance I've ever had. I'd like to turn that around." She looks at Ginni and winks. "Too bad you're so happily married."

Ginni sits back on the sofa. "I'm not so sure about the happily or the married, at the moment."

"What do you mean, pet?" Magpie sits back on the sofa, next to her. "Don't tell me there's trouble in paradise."

"I always know when Nikki is hiding something," Ginni starts letting her feelings pour out. "Especially if the something involves sexual contact."

"Sex!" Magpie asks, genuinely surprised. "You mean the Leftenant is unfaithful?"

Ginni makes a sour face. "Not exactly unfaithful. I don't think she ever goes the full exercise. But I know she gets involved in a few contact sports."

"How do you know?" Magpie wants more information.

"She always looks guilty." Ginni explains. "She gets this stupid grin on her face, which she tries to control because it's so inappropriate to what you're talking about."

Magpie tries not to laugh. "And has she had this grin lately?"

"Yes." Ginni's eyes show more anger than humor. "She had it when she came home from her meeting with Trang. I always knew those two had some unfinished business, and I expected Nikki to tell me what went on at their meeting. All she said was Coleman was not Celine's father, and Trang's not involved in smuggling. Then she grinned for the rest of the night. I'm still waiting to hear what went on, but anything to do with those Vietnam years is still locked inside her, bubbling and searing her insides. She just won't let it go."

Magpie takes her hand. "That's how a lot of them deal with the war. If you keep it in, you can control it, and the war can't hurt you anymore. They think talking about it is like taking the pin out of the grenade. They're only safe when the pin's in." She leans over and kisses Ginni on the cheek. "I don't think there's anyone for Nikki but you."

Ginni smiles, letting the subject drop. "And speaking of romance, where's Barrett?"

"Barrett only comes over when Nikki is going to be home," Magpie says, letting go of Ginni's hand. "That way she might get a glimpse of her, or she can run into her, or they may even get to talk. I thought I could overcome her crush on the Leftenant, but I don't think I have enough charm. She's a good enough girl, but there's no chemistry. Do you know what I mean?"

"Oh yes," Ginni says getting up. "Barrett only has chemistry for Nikki. Fortunately, I don't have to worry about that romance. We just have to wait long enough for Barrett to meet the right person, someone besides Nikki."

Ginni is about to leave the room when Magpie says, almost under her breath, "Now there is someone for me who does have the right chemistry."

Ginni spins around, "Don't tell me it's Nikki. I already need a flyswatter."

"Oh no." Magpie says. "I like the Leftenant, but she doesn't ring my bells. But in all honesty, my agent, Carol Doyle, makes my very heart melt whenever she's near me." Magpie lets her face fall into her hands after this awkward confession.

"Carol Doyle?" Ginni walks back to Magpie. "You never said anything about this before. Isn't she meeting you tomorrow afternoon? Didn't you say she was staying for a few days?"

Magpie looks up at her with a silly smile on her face.

"Yes, it'll be lovely. She's taking me on a picnic because she believes fresh air is good for the cure. Imagine, sunshine, a pastoral setting...and Carol Doyle."

Ginni just shakes her head and says, "I've got to get to that meeting. Nikki should finish her prayer chain calls in a few minutes, and she'll be in to keep you company."

Ginni passes Nikki entering the living room as she's leaving. Grabbing Nikki by one of the loops on her jeans, Ginni tugs her closer for a long, hard kiss. "See you later, baby," Ginni says in a sultry voice, as she exits.

"Now what was that all about?" Nikki thinks out loud, as she goes over to the sofa to sit next to Magpie.

"I think she likes you," Magpie says playfully.

"Good thing," Nikki comments rather sentimentally. "I don't know what I'd do without her."

"Really?" Magpie sees her chance. "You seem to be rather popular with the ladies."

"And what does that mean?" Nikki asks.

"Well...Barrett has never cooled off about you," Magpie ventures slowly. "Plus there's her mother, Trang."

Nikki throws her a quick look. "Barrett is nursing a school-girl crush which I thought was being transferred to you. As for Trang...there's nothing between us."

"Ginni thinks there is," Magpie offers, informationally. "She thinks your war experience is quite a bond."

Nikki answers thoughtfully. "Our war experiences are a bond, a painful bond, hard to break as I'm sure you know. Ginni doesn't have to worry about Trang."

Magpie's facial expression asks, "Why not?"

Nikki stares vacantly at the floor, as she goes on. "We came very close, just recently. We were both ready to hang on to each other until the memories went away. We both thought that we could find an emotion stronger than remembering. But we also realized sex isn't a tool for forgetting. I think we'll always be close, maybe even love each other in a way. But I don't think I'm going to see much more of her. She's involved with her business and her family."

"I think Ginni would like to hear that," Magpie says quietly. Then adds jokingly, "I, myself, would like more lurid details, but I don't suppose they're forthcoming."

Nikki shakes her head, "No," and Magpie cheerfully changes the subject.

"By the way," Magpie chirps. "I haven't just been lying about not working on the case. Since my headaches left, I've been able to use my full brain power."

"I'm not sure there is much of a case left for us," Nikki says. "Max and the police are trying to put it all together. And I think there are too many pieces to this puzzle."

Magpie grabs her arm. "Leftenant, don't you remember anything from your service days? You start with one small item, learn all you can about that before you move on. This morning I was thinking of Joe Buglio. I'm making a chart." She reaches into her pocket and pulls out a small crumpled piece of paper. Unfolding it on the coffee table, she brushes out the wrinkles. At the top of the page is the name Buglio, then a line leading to the words, "Drugs and prostitution". A second line leads from there to "The Sin Club". This is connected by another to "Mob," and then to the name "Luciano Lucky Spatucci".

Nikki reads through the chart and comments, "I can follow everything until I get to the last name. Who's Luciano Spatucci?"

Magpie leans in closer, as if speaking in confidence. In a hushed tone she says, "During the nineteen-sixties, Lucky Spatucci was the godfather of the largest section of Toronto. He was a very important man in the Business. He was also an ardent suitor of a popular local artist...my Aunt Geneva. They went out a great deal, were even seen in all the popular night spots in those days. And even in the mid-eighties, when I went to live with her, they saw each other at least once every two weeks.

He had already suffered one heart attack, so she cooked for him. They didn't go out, but he often spent the whole night."

She pauses and sits back on the sofa again. With a melancholy tone in her voice, she goes on. "He came to see her twice a week when she went into hospital with the cancer. Brought flowers and candy. He'd tell her stories from their old days...cried terribly at the funeral, and..."

She looks at Nikki. "He told me if I ever needed anything to just give him a call. So I thought I'd call him and get some information on Buglio. Maybe we can at least trace the drugs. See if they connect the dots from Coleman to Celine."

"Unless you can talk to him on the phone," Nikki begins her attempt to put Magpie off the chase. "It sounds like too much traveling for you. Plus, I'm not sure that the drugs are the connection."

Magpie is prepared for this tactic. "Mr. Spatucci has a summer home at Thunder Bay, Ontario. That's only about two hours from here, and I can handle a little diversion right now. You may not have noticed, but I'm ready to climb the walls. I'll be careful and pace myself."

She takes a short breath and keeps talking. "Secondly, I realize the drugs may not be the main clue, but they are a starting point, and who knows what other information, a name, a place, a reason, may come out of my conversation with him."

Nikki knows Magpie is probably right. She also thinks it would be wise to check with Max before she says okay. Max will say forget the whole thing and keep Magpie out of the investigation. Nikki's never seen Magpie so happy and sober in the few years she's known her. Between the successful surgery and her interest in the case, she's actually joyful. This is a good thing. So Nikki gives her a light punch on the arm and says, "Go for it! See what you can find out from him. But don't go alone, and the first sign of trouble, you get out of there."

"Great!' Magpie jumps practically into Nikki's lap and plants a juicy kiss on her cheek. "I promise there'll be no trouble. He's always surrounded by bodyguards, and they all have guns."

This doesn't sound reassuring to Nikki.

CHAPTER 18

The Lake Ontario escarpment surrounds Sheridan, New York and helps create a landscape of patterned green hills throughout the countryside. A State Park called Landpark is built in one of these pristine valleys. Large pieces of steel and wood construction art dot the various areas of the park, while the centerpiece is a huge amphitheatre for concerts and plays.

Magpie convinces Carol Doyle that according to a brochure she read, this is an ideal place for lunch. Carol parks her car on a roadway set off from any of the tourist-laden displays and spreads out a plaid stadium blanket under a budding maple tree. The blanket is now edged with the fresh first grass of the season.

Carol insists Magpie just sit on the blanket and watch, as she unpacks the lunch she bought at a local deli. China dishes and silverware are retrieved from her personal picnic basket, along with some non-alcoholic cider. Magpie reads the cider label, and Carol quickly explains, "I wasn't sure if you were on medicine and maybe shouldn't drink."

Magpie isn't listening. She's really studying the beauty of Carol Doyle, painting her in her mind's eye. Creating one of her pastel flowers, symbolizing this woman's perfection.

Carol Doyle is fair-skinned like Magpie, and at five-foot two inches, not much taller. Her full-figured frame is

accentuated by large ample breasts and a small waist.
Her short black hair is peppered with gray, and she has the
proverbial twinkling dark-brown eyes and chubby cheeks. She
likes to laugh and to see others laugh.

Kneeling on the blanket next to the picnic basket, she
gets thoroughly engrossed in taking one plastic container
after another out of the basket, opening each one carefully,
and placing them decoratively in the center of the blanket. At
one point, a loose marinated artichoke escapes the container
and plops on the bib area of her denim jumper leaving a large
oil spot.

"Oh no!" Carol moans, feverishly wiping the spot
with one of the yellow linen napkins. "Never fails, when you
really want to impress someone. What a mess I can make
without even trying."

Magpie just smiles. She isn't paying attention to the
spot because her eyes are drawn to Carol's noticeable
cleavage visible in the v-neck of her tee shirt as she bends
forward. Trying to remember what was said, since a silence is
signaling a response, Magpie answers, "You don't have to
impress me. I mean...you did that a long time ago...I
mean...too bad."

Magpie leans over with her napkin and starts to help
wipe the spot, which is just above Carol's right nipple. "Here,
can I help. Maybe if we wet the napkin."

Carol stops wiping. She looks at Magpie's hand,
which appears frozen to Carol's breast. Then she looks up
into Magpie's eyes. "Any more of that rubbing," she says
enticingly, "And we may not eat lunch."

Magpie quickly pulls her hand off Carol and sits back
on her side of the blanket. Carol serves the meal, and Magpie
pops the cork on the cider, pouring two glasses full. Carol
raises her glass. "A toast to...your head...your health...your
heart."

They clink glasses and each takes a sip of the cider.

Carol continues quietly, "I was so worried...I was afraid, Magpie. I thought I might lose you...and I feel like I hardly know you...and I want to know you." She suddenly stops not sure of what to say next.

"To my good fortune," Magpie raises her glass again, then brings it down and stares at the cider as she says, "I know you were scared. I was scared too. I could see your concern, the night I left for Buffalo. I didn't know what to say. I...I haven't had a friend like you in a long time. And I appreciate how sensitive you are."

"So, you think you know me." Carol says playfully, trying to lighten up the moment.

"You have been my agent for some time now," Magpie explains. "And we have gone out to dinner...and have I ever told you how lovely your eyes are?"

Carol smiles. "No. We haven't told each other many things. Have I ever told you I like your cute little ass."

Magpie pulls her head back with a jerk and laughs. Then she says, "If this is that kind of a discussion, I will have to add that you have the most fantastic breasts I've ever seen."

"Is that why you kept your hand there so long?" Carol says, teasingly. "Maybe we better get back to our usual discussions of art shows and prices of paintings."

Magpie frowns. "I think this may be more important than my career. I've had a lot of time to think about my life in the last few weeks. A lot of time to think without the influence of alcohol. I've come to some conclusions about how I want to spend the rest of it."

"And do you want to share any of those with your agent?" Carol asks.

"Yes, I do." Magpie sips some more cider. "First, I want to live each day in the moment of that day. I don't want to get caught up in the past or the future, just be there in that time and place. Next, I want to spend those moments with someone I care about. Someone I enjoy being with, and who excites and stimulates me."

Carol breaks eye contact and looks down at her plate. "Any idea who that someone is?"

"She's you!" Magpie sings out. "She's been you for a long time. I just never had the nerve to say the words, to hope you might feel the same. But now I feel I have nothing to lose. This is the biggest gamble in my life since I went to the Falklands." She stops talking for a moment, and their eyes meet again as she says. "I think I love you, Carol."

"Quite a gamble," Carol says softly. "I haven't been sensitive or supportive with your surgery, though. I'm about ten days too late."

"I'll gladly give you another chance," Magpie says nearly choking on the words. "I'll let you support me through all the discomforts of old age, and my nightmares, and my depression, and..."

"Okay. Okay. Let's not make it too tempting." Carol interrupts her. "Your offer is just too good to refuse...and I've always wondered what it would be like to make love in that loft you have." She smiles again.

"Does this mean we're going steady?" Magpie jokes.

Carol quickly responds, "I think it means we're engaged. Now who buys the ring?"

Magpie puts her cider down and leans across the blanket to kiss Carol. As they put their arms around each other for a hug, Magpie's knee ends up in the potato salad. She looks down at the mess on her pants and says, "We have so much in common."

❊

Ginni enters the dimly lit kitchen and is surprised to see Nikki in her robe, sipping hot chocolate at the kitchen table. "What's the matter, honey? Couldn't you sleep?" she asks in a concerned voice.

"I waited up for you." Nikki says, getting up and turning the flame up under the tea kettle. "I thought you might like some hot chocolate or tea."

"That's nice," Ginni says throwing her coat over a kitchen chair and moving next to Nikki. "Are you sure you're okay? No nightmares or flashbacks?"

"No nightmares," Nikki says taking Ginni into her arms. "I need to talk to you."

Ginni pushes away, looks concerned, and says, "I hate when you have to talk to me. I really hate these little discussions. Is this an 'I'm in trouble' talk? Or is it a 'I slept with someone' talk? Or is it an 'I'm leaving you for someone else' discussion?"

Nikki is surprised by the choices Ginni presents. "This is a, I came close to sleeping with Trang, but didn't— and not because I love her anyway, but I love you and always will, discussion."

"Oh." Ginni says weakly. "In that case, please pour my chocolate. I'll just sit right next to you..I want to know everything." She steps closer to Nikki. They embrace and kiss, then she says, "Why don't we have these discussions more often?"

After listening to Nikki's details of her afternoon with Trang and the emotions involved with their mutual connection to the Vietnam War, Ginni sits quietly for a few moments. "How is Celine's case going?" she asks.

Nikki tells her about Trang's plan to get her sister and uncle to America by bribing officials through her export business. She also tells her about Magpie's plan to talk to Lucky Spatucci and try to find out more about where Celine's cocaine came from.

"Isn't that rather dangerous for Mary?" Ginni asks.

"I tried to warn her off the plan," Nikki explains. "But you know how into this Magpie is. And she insists she'll be safe because he was a close friend of her Aunt's. She's not going alone. Carol is going with her."

"Where is Mary?" Ginni asks.

"She left a message on the answering machine that she's staying at the motel with Carol," Nikki responds. "And in the morning, Carol will take her to the hospital for her check-up, and then they're off to Thunder Bay and a visit to Mr. Spatucci. At least playing detective keeps her out of trouble."

"So far," Ginni chimes in. "And speaking of trouble, has Max found out why Coleman cracked you on the head and threw you in the water?"

"That still seems to be a mystery," Nikki says snarling. "One of those mysteries that goes all the way back to NAM, and one I may want to forget with the rest of that war."

CHAPTER 19

Thunder Bay is an upper-class beach community along the Canadian side of Lake Erie. Carol Doyle drives her BMW slowly down the paved connecting street, while Magpie tries to find house numbers on the mail posts and gates of the long private driveways.

"There it is, 422!" Magpie practically shouts, waving at a closed iron gate a few yards away. "That must be his house. You might as well pull over."

Carol eases the car onto the patch of concrete in front of the gate. "And how do we get through the locked gate?" she asks, turning to Magpie.

"There should be a bell or intercom, or something," Magpie says, getting out of the car.

Carol joins her as they scan the gate and the red brick pillars on both sides, looking for a way to get the gate open. "Look at that sign," Carol says, pointing to a small plaque on the right-hand side of the gate.

Magpie gets closer and reads aloud, "No trespassers. Private property. Enter at your own risk, grounds are patrolled." She turns back to Carol. "I can understand with his past history, and he is an old man now. He doesn't want people poking around. But I called him, and he said I should come over today.

If we can just find a way to tell him we're here."

Carol notices a lever next to the large latch lock on the gate. She walks over and presses the lever. There's a click, and the gate swings open. The two of them push each of the squeaking sides wide enough for the car to pass through. They drive a few yards, get out and close the gate behind them.

The driveway is lined with pine trees and perfectly spaced peonies in bloom. When they reach within three hundred yards of the main entrance to the house, the driveway ends and they park the car. "I guess this is another safety precaution for Mr. Spatucci." Carol says, opening her door.

"Not the best way to spend your waning years," Magpie replies. "Perhaps his career choice wasn't the best he could make."

Carol crosses in front of the car and joins Magpie. "Are you sure this is safe?" she asks.

"He's a very old man," Magpie answers reassuringly. "And he was a friend of Aunt Geneva's. He sounded pleased I was coming to visit."

"Okay," Carol begins. "But the sign said the grounds were patrolled. Where's the patrol?"

Magpie shrugs, and they start walking toward the house. They are too far away from the car to get back to it, when they hear noises on the gravel behind them and to either side of the circular rose garden in front of the house. Magpie turns slowly. Barreling down behind them is a rottweiler the size of a Guernsey cow. His mouth is open, and his jungle of sharp, white teeth are clearly visible.

She grabs Carol, who is pointing speechlessly to two other rottweilers coming around either end of the garden. They hug each other and both yell at the same time, "Ahhhhhh!"

They close their eyes and hold on to each other as

tightly as they can. "I'm sorry!...," Magpie screams in her shaky voice."

"I love youuuuu!" Carol yells back, as she buries her face in Magpie's shoulder.

They wait for the impact...but nothing happens. A long minute passes, and Magpie opens her eyes. Carol keeps hers closed. The dogs have surrounded them and are in a sit position. "Look at them," Magpie whispers.

Carol opens her eyes and lifts up her head. Two of the dogs growl. Carol and Magpie clutch each other tightly again. "I think we're all right, if we don't move," Magpie says softly.

"And for how long do we hold this position before they eat us," Carol whispers sarcastically.

They continue to shiver in unison as they contemplate their fate. But suddenly, a woman's voice with a slight Spanish accent is heard from the front steps. "C'mon Curly! Jew bad boys! Larry and Moe. Jew too! Bad muchachos! C'mon over here!"

The dogs obediently run to the young woman on the steps wearing the nurse's pant uniform. "I'm sorry," she says, waving to the two women clinging to each other. "Dee muchachos went out to play. I forgot he say you're coming. Come in, come in. Dey no hurt you."

Magpie and Carol are unconvinced but too embarrassed not to follow her into the house. "I'm Carmelita Ortiz, Mr. Spatucci's nurse. I visit three days a week." She leans in, puts her hand to the side of her mouth and speaks confidentially. "I don't really like dee dogs...too much hair. Dat's why I throw dem out. I'm youst about finished with the exam and medicine, so jew can come in." She turns and leads the way down the ceramic-floored hallway to the end room.

They enter a large den. One full wall is a stone fireplace, the opposite wall is covered with taxidermy trophies; a red fox, a colorful pheasant, a large brown rabbit, a deer head with antlers next to a smaller doe head, and a large black boar's head. All seem to stare down from eternity on whoever enters the room. Their glass eyes follow each visitor as she walks across the room.

The wall opposite the door is mostly ceiling to floor window, framing a view of a deep-green, neatly manicured lawn running into the blue of the lake. This is where Lucian Spatucci sits in a dark-brown lounger, an Afghan over his lap, watching the lake flow by. He appears to be the size of a ten-year-old child, dwarfed by the extra pillows behind his back and head. His head is shiny and bald with only a few gray tufts above each ear. His olive-skinned face is clean-shaven and wrinkled, so that he resembles a dried Greek olive.

He smiles when he sees Magpie and weakly waves her forward. "Come in, Mary. Come over, sit on the couch," he says in a barely audible husky voice.

Magpie and Carol obey, moving to the matching sofa next to his chair. Magpie takes a few steps closer and offers her hand. "Uncle Lucky, how have you been?"

He takes her hand in his and pats it with his other hand. "Geneva's girl, the painter. How many years ago. And still such a small girl. It's a nice you come to visit."

The nurse puts her hand on his shoulder and says, "I'm going now. I'll be back on Friday. Remember, no salt, no cigars."

He lets go of Magpie's hand, and she returns to the sofa and sits down. The nurse picks up her bag from a corner table. He waves to her. "Carmelita, on your way out tell Giovanni to bring some coffee and cake for the guests."

Carmelita only gets to the doorway when a tall, muscular man in his early forties enters the room carrying a tray. He's dressed in a beige linen suit with matching slip-on shoes, a long-sleeved, French-cuffed shirt with silver cuff-links, and a muted Calvin Klein tie. He brings the tray up to the coffee table in front of the women and puts it down.

"This is my grandson, Giovanni," Spatucci explains.

"He lives with me now, takes care of all my business and protects me. Isn't he a handsome boy, Mary?"

Not sure how to reply, Mary quickly says, "Oh yes. You must be proud of him. And I'm sure he's a lot of company."

Giovanni winks at her, and Spatucci reminisces, "I remember when I had five or six of the boys with me at all times, day and night. They were the smartest and the best shots. Most of them are gone now. And the children and grandchildren—they just want to go to college, be environmentalists. What the hell is an environmentalist or music therapist. I don't understand this world any more."

He points again to Giovanni, pouring the coffee. "Giovanni's the only one interested in the business now. He's my right hand. You're a good boy, Giovanni. Someday, I'll really show my appreciation."

Carol picks up her coffee and kicks Magpie lightly in the shin. They share a knowing glance before sipping their coffee and tasting the biscotti before them.

Giovanni leaves as quietly as he came, but Magpie knows he's not far away. She introduces Carol as her agent, and they all share stories about Geneva. From time to time a tear escapes Spatucci's eye and trickles down his wrinkled cheek.

Magpie finally sees an opportunity to interject some questions into the conversation. "Uncle Lucky, I didn't come just for the visit, although I've thought of you many times since Aunt Geneva died. I'm helping a friend, and we need some information you might be able to give me."

Spatucci takes a long look at her, then puts his hands together, intertwining his fingers. "I knew there was a problem, Mary. I was afraid you were the one in trouble. I owe your Aunt so much, so much happiness she gave me. So the debt goes down to you. Now what do you want to know?"

"There's a man in Fort Erie, named Joe Buglio. He owns a place called The Sin Club." Because of her nervousness, she starts rambling a little too fast. "One of the girls who danced there, her name was Celine, died of an overdose of cocaine. Well, it wasn't really an overdose. It was pure cocaine, and she probably didn't know that, and so really, she was killed."

He lets her catch her breath, as he comments. "Cocaine is bad business. They put it in their arms, in their nose...bad business."

Magpie starts again. "This Celine was the daughter of a friend of a friend of mine. And this friend, well, she was a Leftenant in the Vietnam War. And her friend was also caught in the war as a civilian deportee. My friend, Nikki, who's also an Episcopal priest, wants to find out who did this. As a matter of fact, some guy named Jimmy Coleman tried to kill her, and then also overdosed on pure cocaine. Is this getting too complicated, Uncle?"

Spatucci sticks his hand down the side of the lounge chair and brings up a large Cuban cigar. He takes a gold lighter out of his bathrobe pocket and lights the cigar, blowing a cloud of smoke around the room. "I'm following most of the story, Mary. Go on."

She takes a deep breath, ready to start again, then more slowly asks, "I wonder if there's any way to find out where the cocaine came from. I thought maybe Joe Buglio would know. Maybe you could find out from him."

"Joe Buglio is bad business," Spatucci says blowing more cigar smoke. "Used to be there was an honor among the businessmen, a personal code. We had families, went to church, knew right from wrong. That's not how it is now, Mary. Joe Buglio is garbage. He likes the young girls, but he gets them hooked on drugs and throws them away. They sent him over here to make absolution for the mess he made in Buffalo. They give him a chance to get back to his wife and kids. They give him a nice restaurant He turns it into a sleazy hall with prostitutes. He's being watched very closely, but still he makes a fool of himself. Greed and fornication, these are the sins that will kill you."

Both Magpie and Carol stare intently as the Don holds court. He takes another long drag on the cigar and goes on. "The story of this girl is already known. Bad business. I'll do a little asking around. I'll try to find out where the drugs came from, how this Jimmy Coleman fits in." He stops smoking and sits up straight. "I have respect for soldiers, Mary. I respect priests too. But this is dangerous business. Your Aunt wouldn't want you involved in this."

Magpie sits up straight. "Aunt Geneva would be proud of me, Uncle. She never turned down a friend...and never missed an adventure. Those are the two things I hope I learned from her."

Carol kicks her again, but Spatucci starts to laugh, a long heart-felt laugh from his very soul. "She did like adventure. Geneva was something else. Let me show you." He carefully pushes back the Afghan and eases himself out of the chair. His bare legs look like fragile twigs that could break at any minute. Bent over, he walks slowly to the fireplace and pushes a button on the right panel. A door opens.

He reaches in and takes out a cut glass carafe and a small picture frame. He shuffles back over to the table and hands the picture to Magpie. "She was so beautiful," he says, emptying the coffee cups back into the decorative pot. "That was taken right here, down by the water." He pours a half-cup of the liqueur in each of the three cups. "So beautiful, she made my heart melt."

Magpie looks at a faded picture of her Aunt at about age twenty-five, wearing a conservative one piece bathing suit, smiling in front of the water. "She always was beautiful," she says softly.

"This is where we had our adventures," he says, his voice cracking. "And now, let's drink to Geneva...." He raises his glass in a toast. "To my beautiful Geneva, my love, my adventure."

They all drink, with Carol coughing on the high-proof

alcohol and Magpie faking a sip. Magpie hands back the photo. "We really need to be getting back."

Spatucci shuffles more slowly to his chair and sits down heavily. He looks at the picture in his hand and sighs. "Of course. I'll call when I have the information you want." Then he looks at the door and raises his voice. "Giovanni! Giovanni! Come and show the ladies to their car." He looks at Magpie and says, "I'm sorry. I'm suddenly very tired. Please excuse me for not showing you out."

Magpie walks over and gives him a hug, kissing his cheek. "I'll come again, Uncle Lucky. I'll come to visit. We can talk about Aunt Geneva some more."

He smiles at her, as Giovanni enters ready to walk them to the car. As they leave the house and start walking across the gravel, Carol ventures a question. "And where are Curly, Larry and Moe?"

Giovanni finally speaks. "They're in with Grandfather right now, sitting by the fireplace, watching him sleep."

"How is he doing?" Magpie asks.

"Not so well," Giovanni answers, opening the car door for her. "He has prostrate cancer. They've done all they can. He's making peace with the world. I think he's ready to go, though. He lost his wife about a year ago and two of his children. He always said you shouldn't outlive your children."

He stops talking and closes the car door. Carol opens her own door and slides behind the wheel. She starts the motor, and they watch Giovanni walk back up to the house. Carol makes a u-turn in the wide drive and heads for the gate. They both get out to push open the heavy Iron doors. Carol drives out and parks, then joins Magpie as they close them again before returning to the car.

"Not what you would expect for the biggest mobster in Toronto," Magpie says.

Carol takes her hand, steering with only one. "We all get old."

"You know, I never realized he had a wife and kids," Magpie continues. "I guess it didn't matter."

Carol squeezes her hand. "I guess not. He loved Geneva, and I think he'll try and help. So the visit was worth it."

"Yeah," Magpie answers. "I'm glad I got to see him again. Maybe Aunt Geneva is the reason I'm involved in this thing after all."

"Well, if she is the reason," Carol says thoughtfully. "Then remind me to thank her tonight. Because if you didn't go to Buffalo and see Ginni about the surgery, and get involved with Nikki's mystery, I probably wouldn't have come down or told you I love you. Nor would I be sleeping with you and talking like you. Is that why they call you Magpie?"

Magpie leans over and kisses Carol on the neck. "Yes, I believe I get excited and never know when to stop."

"We'll see," Carol says, and they both laugh.

CHAPTER 20

Nikki reaches over her desk to answer the office phone. She's been working steadily for the last two hours on her fall lesson plans and doesn't mind a little diversion. "Professor Barnes," she says into the receiver.

"Look Barnes, you were interested in some information about Jimmy and that girl," Darla. Coleman says nervously. "You need information, and I need money. I need some new clothes and a one-way ticket to California."

Nikki touches the scar on her forehead and smooths back the white streak of hair just above it. "What makes you think your information is worth any money?" she says cautiously.

"Maybe you're not as interested as I heard you were." Darla says sarcastically. "Jimmy did crack your head open, didn't he?"

"He tried to kill me!" Nikki shoots back. "And I already know everything you told the police, and it isn't worth any money."

Darla gives a little laugh, then says, "This isn't what I told the police. This is new information about where Jimmy

got his stash. I got a name, and it's a big name. If you don't
want to know who it is, I can always go to the source and get
some cash for keeping quiet. I was just trying to do the right
thing."

She has Nikki's full attention. "How much is it going
to cost me for you to do the right thing?" Nikki snipes.

"One thousand dollars," Darla snaps back. "That
should just about cover my expenses."

"I don't have a thousand dollars," Nikki says.
"Especially for information I may not be able to trust."

"This ain't no garage sale," Darla retorts. "One
thousand dollars, bring it to the pool room on Clinton and
Jefferson tonight at eight. I'll only wait until eight-fifteen.
Then it goes to the next customer." She hangs up.

"Wait! I need more time to get...," Nikki's talking to a
dead line. She slams down the phone in frustration and slaps
the top of her desk.

In less than a moment, she picks up the phone again
and dials Max's number. Her frustration rises again as she
tries to explain her conversation with Mrs. Coleman. "Can't
you have her arrested or at least brought in on extortion or
something?" Nikki asks.

"Nope." Max answers back. "She can say you just
wanted to give her some money...or doesn't know what
you're talking about...has no information." He thinks for a
minute. "She may really have something. Information would
get to her before either of us."

"Are you saying I should meet her and pay the
money?" Nikki asks.

"That's always a dangerous job," Max says, adding,
"And that's a bad neighborhood. But I could go with or have
a plainclothes officer get there before you. Only problem,
Nikki...we don't have that kind of money for informers. My
budget is down to zero."

"I can get the money," Nikki says tenuously. "I guess
the payoff is worth doing if we even get one small piece of
information.

I'm just so pissed at Mrs. Coleman and her money-hungry morality."

"Don't be too hard on her," Max says, trying to be reassuring. "She doesn't have anything anymore. Jimmy was her meal ticket, now he's gone. This is probably the only legacy he'll leave."

Nikki listens to what Max is saying and to all the innuendoes in his words. She should have thought about some of this too, before she got angry. Poverty and what it drives people to do is often forgotten when you're in a comfortable position. Finally calming down, she says, "I see what you mean, Max. So, have somebody there just for backup if I need him. I'll call as soon as I have the information."

They hang up, and Nikki searches her brain for where to get the money. There's two thousand dollars in her and Ginni's vacation fund, but she doesn't want to ask Ginni for the money. She doesn't even want Ginni to know what she's doing. There's no need to make her worry.

She decides to call Trang. After all, Trang has as much of a vested interest in the information as Nikki does. And Trang can get her hands on that much money in a short amount of time, and that's about how long Nikki has.

Trang agrees to get the money and give it to Nikki, but not until Nikki agrees that she can come along.

❁

Nikki picks Trang up at her home in North Buffalo at seven. They go to the pool hall in Nikki's car, which is less conspicuous than Trang's Mercedes. Nikki wears her jeans and an old St. David University sweatshirt. Trang takes Nikki's advice and also dresses in jeans and a yellow tank top. Her straight black hair is worn loose and down.

As she gets out of the car, Nikki finds she's controlling her hormones again.

They walk into the Jefferson Avenue Pool Parlor, and the first thing to hit them is the smell. A mixture of beer, old cigarettes, and urine that have been blending together for some time. They both squint their eyes, trying to adjust to the dim lighting and thick smoke. The Parlor is basically two rooms. You enter from outside into the bar room, a fifteen by fifteen foot room crammed with five tables, each surrounded with chairs. The bar is only five feet from the door, plain and box-like with what looks like a linoleum top. Six stools are in front with only two occupied.

The heavy-set African-American bartender and the two gray-haired African-American customers look at the women as they enter. The five other customers, scattered at several tables, also stop talking and look at the women.

Nikki and Trang cross in front of the bar and move to the back room. This room is about the same size as the barroom but houses four pool tables. At the far table, a forty-year-old African-American man wearing a flannel shirt with the elbows worn through and a Yankee's baseball cap, shoots pool alone. At the other end of the room stands Darla Coleman in a red mini-skirt and short black top baring her stomach. She nervously huddles into the corner, smirking with relish.

Nikki and Trang move over to her. Nikki speaks first, "I'm Nikki Barnes. Do you have the information?"

"Who's that?" Mrs. Coleman waves her lit cigarette toward Trang. "She a cop?"

"No." Nikki answers quickly. "She's my girlfriend...didn't want me to come alone."

"She better not be a cop," Mrs. Coleman says nervously, looking at the two women. "I guess you do look like a couple of dykes. So where's the money?"

Trang, not saying anything, opens her shoulder bag and lifts a wad of bills half-way out. Then she quickly puts them back and closes the flap on the purse.

"First the information," Nikki says. "Then the money."

Mrs. Coleman very deliberately drops her cigarette on the floor and grinds it out with her high-heeled shoe. She looks at Nikki and smugly says, "First the money or no information."

Nikki nods to Trang, who goes into the purse again, retrieves the money, and hands it to Mrs. Coleman; who snatches it up quickly and puts it in her own small evening bag.

Darla leans in toward Nikki and says, "Now I'm only going to say this once. I talk, and I'm outta here. Jimmy told people, reliable people, that the girl got a shitload of good stuff from her daddy. You know...her old man, and I don't mean her boyfriend...." She looks at a rear door and back to Nikki. "Meaning, she got the stuff from that Fairburn guy, her rich stepfather. Maybe that wasn't the only time he supplied her or Jimmy. Know what I mean? Maybe her step-daddy bought'em the hot shots too."

She pats her small purse and turns, walking quickly to the back door. She's gone in less than a minute. Nikki looks at Trang, whose face reflects anger and confusion. Neither speak as they cross back in front of the bar and out the front door. They start walking the block to Nikki's car, when they realize the African-American man playing pool is behind them. Nikki moves closer to Trang, and they quicken their steps. They reach the car and Nikki unlocks Trang's door. As she goes to open it, the man reaches over and pushes the door closed.

"Sergeant Mullen's in the car across the street," he says to Nikki.

Looking over, Nikki sees Max smiling in the front seat of an older model Chevy. She finishes closing Trang's door and locks the car. Then she and the pool player cross the street to talk to Max.

"So, how'd it go?" He asks Nikki as the pool player gets into the driver's seat.

"Thanks for the back-up, Max" she says patting the arm he's resting on the open window. "We got information all right. I'm still not sure how much it can be trusted."

"Why not let me judge," Max encourages her on.

"Coleman's wife swears by her sources that Douglas Fairburn gave drugs to his daughter. Mrs. Coleman also hinted that she thought maybe the stepfather gave them the fatal overdoses." Nikki stops talking, looking to Max for help.

Max shakes his head. "Those are some accusations...but worth looking into. I'll call Ed Meyers with the Buffalo P.D. and see if I can go with him to talk to Mr. Fairburn. I should be able to tell you what he said sometime tomorrow." He looks across the street at her car. "Do you want us to follow you home?"

"There's no need to," Nikki answers. "Trang furnished the money. I'll drive her home to North Buffalo; then I'll head straight to Sheridan."

Max gives her a light punch in the arm and says goodbye. Nikki goes back across the street, gets into her car, and heads for North Buffalo.

✄

Nikki enters the Elm Street arterial heading for the connecting entrance to the mainline. She turns on her signal light, but before she can turn Trang touches her arm and says, "I want to go to the Fairburn Building. You can drop me there."

"Isn't it rather late to go to the office?" Nikki asks, pulling back into traffic. "Don't you think an empty building is a little dangerous, this late at night?" She asks again, trying to uncover the real motive for Trang going there.

"We have security guards there all night," Trang answers, trying to evade the real question. "At Fairburn Enterprises, people often work through the night, especially if they are waiting for an overseas fax or phone call."

They drive in silence until they reach the lit entrance to the building. Nikki wants to reassure Trang before they separate. "Thanks for the money," she says hesitantly. "I'm not sure we can believe anything she said. You understand that, don't you?"

"Of course," Trang says flatly. "Your friend, Max, will check it all out and let you know. And you will call me." She opens the car door. "Now I really should do some work. I'll have a cab take me home. Good night."

She closes the car door and walks to the lit building entrance. Nikki watches her knock on the large glass doors. A security guard recognizes her and unlocks the door, letting her in. When they're both out of sight, Nikki follows the curved driveway and cuts through the parking lot. There are only three cars parked in the large lot. An old Plymouth, a Ford van, and a new Cadillac.

She exits the parking lot and gets to the first red light on the adjoining street. She's preoccupied with how Trang must feel after hearing Douglas might be involved with the drugs that killed Celine. The light changes to green, but Nikki doesn't move. *Who else might be working this late at Fairburn enterprises? Who would own a Cadillac?* A delivery truck honks its horn behind her, and she instinctively lunges the car forward. Then she quickly makes a u-turn and heads back to the parking lot.

"Trang knew Douglas was working tonight," she says aloud to herself. "That's why she wanted to go to the office."

She speeds back down the entranceway drive, slamming on her brakes at the front doors. Running up to the glass doors, she pounds on them with her open hands. The Security Guard, hand on his holstered gun, cautiously approaches and asks through the locked door, "Who are you? What do you want?"

Nikki quickly tries to think of a reason that will gain

her entrance to the building. "I'm Reverend Barnes...." She fumbles in her pocket for her wallet and some identification. Flipping it open to her driver's license with her picture in her clerical collar, she pushes the wallet up to the window. "I just dropped Mrs. Fairburn off, but I forgot to check an appointment with her. I'd like to see her...just for a moment."

The guard studies the picture. The clothes and title on the license convince him to relax his hold on his gun. He opens the door grumbling, "She said she'd be in her office. I hope you know your way up there. I can't leave my post, Lou's making floor rounds."

"I know where it is," Nikki says confidently, trying to reassure him. "And I notice Mr. Fairburn's car is in the lot. Is he still working too?" She tries to sound casual.

"Mr. Fairburn's been working on the gardens all week," the guard replies in a disinterested tone. "If you want to see him, you'll have to go to the atrium." He points to the large glassed foyer behind the smaller one they're standing in.

"Well maybe I should just say hello to him first," Nikki says nonchalantly, heading for the atrium.

The guard just shrugs and returns to the open newspaper on his station desk. Nikki takes quick long strides as she crosses the first foyer. She slows her pace as she enters the arboretum, the smell of dirt and greenery mixes with the sound of the large waterfall. Following the sound of the water, she works her way around the outer rim of plants.

Just past the three-story waterfall, she sees them, Trang and Douglas. He's kneeling in a hydrangea bed, a small trowel in one gloved hand, a potted border plant in the other. She's on the sidewalk, clutching her purse with both hands, anger apparent in her face.

Nikki moves close enough to hear what they're saying. Because of the intensity of their conversation and the leafy foliage that precedes the hydrangea bed, Nikki is unnoticed.

"Did you Douglas? I want the truth!" Trang demands. Douglas doesn't face her. He continues digging a hole for the small plant. "That's ridiculous," he says dismissively. "Where did you hear something like that from your Army friend?"

Trang moves closer to him, her voice demanding attention. "Did you give her and that Coleman drugs? I want to know the truth!"

This time he turns to her. "Do you think I would be that base? Is that what you think of me?"

"It doesn't matter what I think of you," Trang shoots back. "I want to know the truth. Just for once, try to tell the truth. Did you ever give her drugs."

He turns away again but doesn't resume his work. Staring at one of the blooming bushes, he says hesitantly, "I was pretty bad for awhile. You know that Trang." He looks at her. "I was under so much pressure. The habit was just too much for me. Celine used to beg me for a little taste, just for recreation...I swear, I never did it with her...I just gave her a little, for her and her friends...maybe only twice. And that was before I went to the clinic. I was pretty high myself... not thinking straight."

Trang hardens her face, puts her hand in her purse and pulls out the 9MM, pointing it at Douglas. "I should have left years ago," she says, biting each word with anger. "I should have taken the children and left. I thought a family would be better for them, that the money would help them, maybe bring them success. I thought you were through with the drugs. You kept promising and promising." She holds the gun with two hands and points it at his head.

Nikki moves quickly, "Trang! No! You can't do this!" She runs toward her.

Trang holds Douglas's frightened look with her own angry stare. "I am going to kill you. I only wish I could do it with the cocaine instead of this gun."

"Do you hate me that much," he says in an even calm voice. "Have I hurt you so much, you could do this?"

Nikki grabs Trang's wrist, forcing down the hand with the gun. "You can't do this!" she says, as they struggle for control of the gun. "You can't shoot him!" Nikki tries to make her listen.

Trang stops struggling but doesn't give up the gun. She looks at Nikki and says, "I <u>can</u> do this. He killed Celine. He couldn't keep his filthy habit to himself, couldn't just kill himself slowly with the drugs. He had to give them to her."

"I didn't kill her!" Douglas says adamantly, dropping the trowel and plant and getting up. "You have to believe that!" He walks over to Trang. "I wouldn't hurt her. I loved Celine. I loved her. She was my daughter."

He's only a foot away from Trang. He begins sobbing, burying his face in his hands. Nikki still holds onto the gun in Trang's hand, but they no longer struggle. Trang lets go of the gun, and Nikki pulls it away. Trang, still looking at Douglas, says to Nikki, "You can take the gun, but I will avenge Celine's death."

"I didn't kill her!" Douglas screams, looking up at her. "I did give her drugs but only twice. She had her own supplier. I even bought drugs from her supplier."

"Who was it?" Nikki demands, as she turns to face him. "Who was her supplier?"

"I...I don't think I should tell you," he hesitates.

"Why?" Trang steps closer to him...stares at him for a moment...then with all her strength slaps his face. "Why? Are you afraid you still might need to get drugs from him. Are you afraid of losing your own source, even if that person is responsible for your daughter's death."

He holds the slapped cheek with his hand and says, "Her name is Kimberly Remington. She was a friend of Celine's."

Trang backs away from him and turns to Nikki. "I know this girl, always hanging around with Celine, always encouraging her to go out and party." She turns back to Douglas. "Don't come home tonight. Stay here or at a hotel. I don't care where but don't come home. I don't want to see you." Then she walks past Nikki, quietly asking, "Will you take me home. I need to get out of here."

Nikki puts the gun in her belt under her blazer and joins Trang, walking toward the outer foyer and the exit doors. They leave Douglas standing in the arboretum. He's yelling, "Trang wait! Let me try to explain! Trang!"

His words are drowned out by the sound of the waterfall crashing against the boulders below.

※

Once the car is moving toward North Buffalo, Trang looks out the side window and says,
"I don't even know whether to believe him or not. How could he give that poison to Celine!" Her voice cracks. "I knew his habit was getting worse. I always knew when it was happening, and I would tell him to sign himself in somewhere. We talked about Celine and her behavior, and he promised me she was just experimenting. That she'd never get hooked."

She turns to Nikki. "He was so full of the drugs, he didn't know what was real or not. But I should have known it was cocaine talking, not him."

Nikki looks straight ahead and says, "And maybe it was the cocaine that made him give her the drugs."

"There's no excuse for what he did!" Trang says angrily. "I will never forgive him, and I never want to see him again. He is dead to me."

Nikki recognizes this tone of anger and hate. She knows it can't be changed when it's this strong. She tries to move the discussion somewhere else. "What about Kimberly Remington?"

"She's an evil person." Trang says, dispassionate again. "I disliked her from the first time I met her. She comes from wealthy parents, yet she constantly desires more.

Kimberly Remington could easily be a murderer. I have always found her empty of remorse or love for that matter. She works in an expensive dress boutique on Delaware Avenue."

Trang pauses, then asks, "If we go to talk to her, do the police have to know?"

Nikki looks at her, "Not if we just go to talk to her...and I keep the gun."

There's silence again, as Nikki drives down the long driveway of the Fairburn home. Trang opens the car door and steps out. Then she bends down, and says to Nikki, "I'll behave myself. You have my word. I just want to know the truth."

"We can talk to her tomorrow...but just talk. I'll be here by noon. Is that okay?" Nikki asks hesitantly.

"Yes. I understand. Noon is fine," Trang answers meekly, then turns and walks toward her door.

Nikki heads her car for home. Feeling uncomfortable about not telling Max this new information. She justifies her actions out loud. "He'll find out the same thing when he questions Fairburn tomorrow...then he'll find out that I already know. I just hope he doesn't find out about Trang and the gun."

As she ends this conversation with herself, she takes the gun out of her belt, where she tucked it, and puts it in the glove compartment of the car.

Trang will somehow get to question Kimberly Remington, whether the police know about Remington's connection to the murders or not. But Nikki's not sure how Trang will react if she finds out the connection is a major one. Her reason is telling her to call Max, but her heart is telling her to support Trang. She decides to wait until after they talk to Remington to call Max.

CHAPTER 21

The Bon Ami is a small upscale dress shop tucked in between a jewelers and a cafe on a one block stretch just past the tall office buildings of Delaware Ave. The street parking is limited, but Nikki finds a space in front of the cafe and glides her car to the curb.

Nikki decides to dress more professionally for this interview, since professional clothes in this neighborhood may carry more power than jeans. She wears her baggy double-breasted black pantsuit and a white, band-collar blouse.

Trang is also dressed in black. She wears a knee-length business suit and shorter, one-inch heels. They enter the dress shop together, and Trang scans the long room, looking for Kimberly Remington. She inconspicuously nods to a twenty-five-year-old woman talking to a customer by the scarves display.

They walk over, and Nikki tries to appear interested in the scarves while the young woman finishes with the customer. Trang just stands and stares at Kimberly, who finally sees Trang and gives her a knowing glance, telling the customer. "You can just pay for that at the front counter."

The customer leaves, and Kimberly ignores Trang by walking up to Nikki. "Can I help you sir? Oh, I'm sorry, madam."

"Yes," Nikki begins. "You can help me and Mrs. Fairburn. Shall we talk here or somewhere less public?"

The thin, five-foot-eight woman flips her shoulder-length, dyed ash-blonde hair over the shoulder of her bright-red, Donna Karen jersey dress. "I don't have to answer any questions from either of you." She touches her lip with her long, color-coordinated to her dress, perfectly manicured nail. And still ignoring Trang, says to Nikki, "Who are you anyway?"

Time to haul out the title, although it may not affect this one, Nikki thinks to herself. "I'm Reverend Nikki Barnes, an old friend of Mrs. Fairburn and Celine."

"Yeah...," Kimberly feigns sadness. "Too bad about Celine. I tried to tell her to cut down on that shit...but you know she just wouldn't."

After this last remark, Trang loses her temper. She grabs Kimberly's arm and whirls her around . Now face to face, Trang spews out her question, "Did you give her the drugs? Did you supply her?"

Kimberly tugs her arm away from Trang. "Shhh! What's the matter with you. Keep your voice down will you?"

Trang moves closer, and Nikki knows another slap is coming. This one aimed at Kimberly. She steps between them to block the blow and says firmly to Kimberly, "I asked you before, shall we talk here or go someplace less public?"

"Okay. Okay," Kimberly whines. "I'll take my break. We can go next door. But you've got a hell of a nerve coming in here...."

Nikki cuts her off. "You've got a hell of a nerve selling drugs. So don't think this is a social visit."

Kimberly glares at her but says nothing. She walks to the front counter with Nikki and Trang close behind.

"I'm taking my break," she announces to the older cashier, who just nods.

They walk next door and sit at one of the outside tables. A waiter appears, and Nikki orders three coffees. Kimberly interrupts the order and in a condescending voice says, "I don't drink caffeine. I'll have a spring water please with ice."

Trang loses all tolerance for this woman. She reaches across the small round table and grabs Kimberly's arm again. "Did you give Celine drugs? Did you get them for her?"

Kimberly tries to pull away, but Trang won't let her. "Let go of me! You can't do this to me! I don't have to answer any questions!" Kimberly protests.

Nikki has had enough too. She grabs Kimberly's other arm. "Yes. You do have to answer our questions. And when you're done answering ours, I'm sure the police will have some too."

Kimberly stops struggling. "Now listen," she says, trying to shrug lose from their hold on her. "I don't really need to talk to any police." Nikki and Trang let go of her arms, as she continues, "I'm sorry about Celine, but she did have a bad habit. I was only doing her a favor because she was a friend, you know."

Trang glares with anger at her but says nothing. Kimberly goes on, "I never sold her stuff. I never made any money off my friends. When Celine got really bad and couldn't score with any of her other sources, and she had plenty to choose from at that club in Fort Erie. Anyway, when she was really desperate, what could I do, she was my friend. So then I copped for her."

"Did you get her the last stuff she bought?" Nikki asks, stressing the seriousness of the situation in her tone of voice. "Did you give her the cocaine she had the night she died?"

Kimberly is noticeably nervous now. She continuously pushes her hair back over her ears. "Look, I don't need any trouble right now. My father is talking about throwing me out. I can't get in any trouble," she stutters on.

"You're already in trouble!" Nikki practically yells at her. "You may be arrested for murder. Will your father like that?"

"Murder! Come on now!" she stops playing with her hair and starts pulling at her nails. "I didn't have anything to do with any murder...I gave Celine the same stuff Benny gave me. I didn't even have to pay for it. Benny gave it to me...said he liked Celine too. He was going to bring it over to her himself."

"Did he?" Trang growls. "Did he bring the cocaine to Fort Erie?"

"No," Kimberly answers pleadingly. "Look, he did it as a favor. Celine was in bad shape. I told him, I needed stuff right away. I told him I had to get it to her. She didn't trust anyone but me."

"You brought it to her?" Trang asks.

"Yeah," she says, her voice cracking. "But it was good stuff, I swear! I snorted a line with Benny before I brought the rest over to her."

Nikki hunts for more information. She asks, "Were they in separate packages?"

"Yeah, of course...," Kimberly's confusion is apparent. "But they always come in separate packages. What are you saying...look I can't get involved in this."

"Well you're already involved!" Trang shoots back. "You gave her the drugs that killed her. That makes you very involved." She takes a breath, then demands, "Who is this Benny? Where can we find him?"

"I...I...don't think I should tell you...," Kimberly stutters.

Nikki grabs her arm again. "I think you better tell us. And I think you better call the police as soon as we leave and explain your involvement in this...or you may be going to jail."

Kimberly's eyes grow wider, as she says slowly, "His name is Benjamin Conti. He was my boyfriend for awhile. I always meet him at the Castaway Bar on the waterfront. But listen, don't tell him I told you? Okay? I don't want to get a bad reputation down there."

"I wouldn't worry about your reputation," Nikki says, standing up. "I'd worry more about your prison sentence for accomplice to murder." She motions Trang, who steels herself and stands too.

Nikki takes a few steps toward the car, but Trang stays at the table and stares at Kimberly.
"Trang!" Nikki calls to her, fearing she's ready to hit again.

Trang's expression changes from anger to contempt. She leans over the table and spits on Kimberly's face. Kimberly jumps and screams, feverishly wiping the spit off her face, as Trang says, "That's for your friendship. That's how much it was worth."

Nikki rushes back, grabs Trang, and hurries her to the car. She pulls open the car door and pushes Trang into the seat. Trang is unemotional now. Turning to look up at Nikki, she says, "I forgot my purse...back at the table."

Nikki slams the car door and stomps quickly back to the table. Kimberly is already half-way to the cafe ladies room. Nikki snatches the purse off the table and bolts back to the car. She gets in the driver's seat, plops the purse on Trang's lap, and pulls away from the curb just in time to see a police car pull up in front of the dress shop.

Nikki looks over her shoulder and sees Max get out of the back seat. "That's Max with the Buffalo Police," she remarks to Trang. They keep driving down the street. "They must have talked to Douglas, and he told them about Kimberly. In the state we just left her, she's bound to tell them about Benjamin Conti. I don't think we should try to find him. I think we should let Max handle him. I'll connect with Max later and let you know what happens."

Trang is silent for a few minutes. Finally, she says in a tired voice, "I don't have the energy to see anyone else today, anyway. My poor Celine. How did she stray so far. Was she so unhappy not knowing who she was?" She looks at her hands. Her knuckles are white from clutching her purse so tightly. "I didn't want her to remember the struggle to get to America. I wanted her to be the daughter of a rich respected diplomat and businessman. Now I think I should have told her she was some sex-hot soldier's bastard, and her mother was nothing but a fucking prostitute."

Each word hits Nikki like the Viet Cong bullets she took at the Xuan Loc ambush. She pulls the car over to the curb, grabs Trang's shoulders and shakes her, saying, "Don't ever say that about yourself! Don't ever let them win that battle! You survived because you had to, any way you had to. You saved your baby."

Nikki starts crying now, crying and talking at the same time. "They shouldn't have done this to you. They never should have touched you. Vietnam was a dirty war that achieved nothing but raping women like you, raping a beautiful land and culture. Trang, don't let them conquer your mind now. You've fought them for so long."

Nikki wraps her arms around Trang. Through her tears, she says, "Remember who you really are, and who you fought to become. Don't let them win this war. You have the victory. You are the victory."

Trang holds Nikki closer, letting her cry. She consoles Nikki saying, "I won't give up. Celine is lost, but I am still alive. And I believe I am alive for some reason. I won't be a victim again, Nikki. I fought too hard. I am okay now, my woman soldier. But you need to absolve yourself. All the sins of the U.S. Army were not yours."

Nikki breaks from the embrace and sits back, trying to compose herself. Taking a tissue out of her pocket, she wipes her eyes and nose and puts the car in gear. In silence, they drive to Trang's North Buffalo home again. They park by the front door. Trang sighs deeply and finally relaxes her shoulders. "There are so many people involved in her murder. I don't know what to think any more," she finally says.

Trang's exhaustion is apparent, as she continues, "I have to leave for Vietnam in a few days. I'm making the last delivery of money. All the negotiations could easily fall apart if something goes wrong. I need to keep the police and government officials from being too nosy."

She puts her hand on Nikki's arm. "I trust you to find out who murdered my daughter. I promised her in a dream the night she died, that I will avenge her life and her death. But I must also consider those living now. My uncle and my sister deserve a chance to be free and out of pain for whatever time they have left. Barrett and my family are all I have left...and you, Nikki. Will you find the murderer and let me know who did this?"

"I promise you," Nikki says. "I'll find out who did this, and I'll see that justice is done. I'll call you right after I talk to Max. If Conti is the killer, you'll know as soon as I do."

Trang reaches over and touches Nikki's lips. Then she leans in and kisses Nikki's lips softly. Nikki kisses back. Looking into Trang's eyes, she sees them wash over with tears, as if some deep emotion is drowning within her. Trang quickly opens the car door and walks toward her house.

Nikki feels her eyes welling up again, as she pulls out of the driveway and heads for home.

CHAPTER 22

"Of course I was going to call you, Max!" Nikki lies, as she speaks into the receiver. Knowing full well Max knows she's lying.

"And when was that gonna be?" he asks sarcastically. "After Trang blew her husband's brains out or after she shot the Remington girl, or maybe after this Conti guy threw the two of you in the lake."

"I took the gun away from her. She was just upset. She didn't hurt anyone." Nikki tries to defend Trang.

"Well according to the blubbering husband, she doesn't think much of him as a man, and he shoulda let her shoot him," Max hammers on. "So was she gonna use a water pistol or is that 9MM still floating around?"

Nikki tries to sound repentant. "I have it in my car. But you can understand how upset she was. Her husband was giving drugs to her daughter. You have to admit, that can make you a little crazy."

Max calms down. "I can't afford her being crazy. It's too dangerous for her...and for you. This Conti is a dope-head of the first magnitude."

"She's not going to get involved anymore." Nikki tries to sound convincing. "I had a long talk with her. She's out of the case. I told her I'd keep her informed...whenever you give me information."

"I hope you're right, Nikki," Max warns her. "This case is growing and growing. We got more suspects than murders, and they all come from different circles of society. But they all have one thing in common, using and abusing drugs. Which makes each of them unpredictable and dangerous."

"So you want me to keep my nose out of the case, too," Nikki asks sheepishly. "I guess you don't have to tell me what you found out about Conti and the drugs he gave to Celine."

"If you're sure Trang is calmed down and staying out of the investigation," Max gives in. "Then I guess you can come with me while they interrogate him. Conti and his lawyer will be in Meyer's office at nine tomorrow morning. We can have a front row seat, if you want to come."

Nikki doesn't hesitate. "I'll be ready at eight. I'll even buy coffee on the way there...." She's suddenly gets very serious, as she says, "Thanks Max. I'm sorry for the poor judgment."

"Yeah. Yeah." Max tries to break the tension. "Just remember two donuts go with that coffee. Bye Nick." He hangs up.

⁂

Nikki hangs up the phone in her bedroom and walks to the window. She's exhausted from the eruption of her emotions earlier in the day when she was with Trang. The two murders have brought back the Vietnam horror she tries to keep buried. They also remind her of the tenuousness of life, the young, lost Celine and the down-on-his-luck musician, Jimmy Coleman. She came so close to being killed, just because of her concern over Celine's death. A shiver slides down her spine. She's well aware of the reality the complicated web spun by Celine's death has her in. Locked into a puzzling corner, she waits for the spider to get caught by the police or come back for supper.

As she stares out the window at a red maple just budding, Ginni knocks on the door and enters the bedroom. Nikki turns and smiles, and Ginni comes up and gives her a kiss on the cheek. "How about going out for dinner?" Ginni says. "I'm up for our little Italian restaurant by the University."

"I thought you had a consultation tonight?" Nikki asks quizzically.

Ginni wraps her arms around Nikki's waist and says, "I did it by phone this afternoon. I've cleared my book and written Nikki across the whole evening. What do you think? Are you ready for ravioli and watching a candle melt on an old Chianti bottle?"

"Is this a romantic liaison or just what the doctor ordered for a mixed up and depressed veteran?" Nikki asks, half-joking.

Ginni hugs her tighter and says, "A little of both. We haven't spent much time together since this whole murder case began. And I haven't kissed your boo boo very much," She bends her head down and kisses Nikki's latest forehead scar. "How will it ever heal?" She smiles.

Nikki gets very serious. Looking into Ginni's eyes, she says, "Whenever I'm with you, I feel as if I'm healing—my past, my body, even my heart." She pauses. "You know you're the one I love, don't you Ginni? I never want to hurt you, especially with some of the unfinished business in my life.

"I do know that," Ginni answers. "And I try to remember all those ghosts you keep hidden away. So when they come out, I can name them 'Vietnam' and wait for them to battle again and go away. I love you, Nikki, and I trust you...even if you do have an odd assortment of women trying to get you in bed."

"There's only one woman I want to go to bed with," Nikki goes on in a lighter mood. "And she's right in my arms as we speak."

"Do you think we could get those ravioli first?" Ginni says wrinkling up her face. "I hate to be practical instead of romantic, but I haven't eaten since breakfast."

Nikki breaks the embrace and takes her hand. "Then let's go!" She starts leading her toward the door.

"Nikki," Ginni gets her attention again. "I really do understand this Trang business. I even understand how you got involved with another murder case. I just worry about you. There's so many crazy people out there."

Nikki stops and gives her a long, meaningful kiss. "Thanks. Hearing you say that means a lot to me...now let's go eat."

CHAPTER 23

Magpie finishes her talk on the use of photography as an adjunct to her paintings. While acknowledging the applause, she walks through the room full of people to her table. Her ankle length teal knit dress sways slightly as she walks, showing off her slender figure. Her small features are accentuated by the subtle make-up she's wearing. A gold wide-brimmed felt hat sits rakishly to one side of her head, covering the scar and bald patch left by her surgery.

Carol Doyle, Clifton Farber, the Chairman of the Albright Art Gallery Membership Committee, and Raymond Fong, President of the Buffalo Watercolor Society all stand, as she returns to her seat at their table. She sits down and quickly drinks most of the water in the glass by her plate.

Mr. Fong makes his way to the podium, and Carol leans over and whispers, "Are you feeling okay. This isn't too tiring, is it? We can always leave."

Magpie shakes her head 'no' and turns her chair to face the podium. Mr. Fong begins his talk on the creative use of color and imagery in Magpie's paintings.

Carol turns her chair more, leans over to Magpie, and again whispers, "Your talk was great!"

Magpie takes Carol's hand and gives it a squeeze before letting go of it.

Mr. Fong finishes his speech and again everyone
stands for Magpie. Mr. Farber then invites everyone into the
gallery for after-dinner refreshments and a private viewing of
Magpie's show. The guests mill around various paintings, and
Magpie and Carol try to move from one group to another.
Several people want to purchase different pieces, and Carol
jots down necessary information.

By eleven o'clock most of the guests have left, and
Carol and Magpie move out to the back stairs for some air.
The Greco-Roman columns and white granite stairs are
washed in the bright moonlight. Carol sits next to a column
and makes notes in her leather-covered pocket notebook.

"Your doing very well with sales, " she says, not
looking up.

Mr. Farber coughs from the top stair, getting their
attention. "I know it's late, but the husband of one of our
members called me several times and drove over from
Canada this evening. He's very anxious to purchase one of
your paintings as a gift for his wife. She was at the show last
week and fell in love with 'Lilies in the Corn Field'. He was
afraid someone would purchase it tonight, so I told him you'd
see him in my office...if you don't mind. It won't take long,
and the 'sold to' sign will be his birthday surprise tomorrow."

Magpie looks at Carol and under her breath says,
"That one's priced at ten thousand dollars."

Carol nods and gets up. "Of course we'll see him, "
she says smiling at Farber.

They make their way back into the gallery. The two
guards are walking room to room, dimming the lights in
preparation for locking up for the evening. The bright track
lighting in the hallways is also being shut down. Only small
security lights at the end of each hallway are left to guide the
guards on their rounds.

Farber's office is brightly lit and the door is open. The

hall leading into the row of offices is also still lit. Farber enters first, then Magpie and Carol make their way into the room. Farber points to a rotund man sitting in his comfortable leather desk chair and says, "Mr. Buglio, I'd like you to meet the artist, Mary York, and her agent, Carol Doyle."

Magpie freezes for a moment, her mind clicking. *How much of her did he really see that night at The Sin Club?* She wonders to herself.

Carol has also made the connection to his name and takes over control. She steps in front of Magpie, offering Buglio her hand. Carol's all business as she says crisply, "Mr. Buglio, how nice of you to come out so late. I hear you're interested in making a purchase."

He takes a fast look at Magpie, his expression seems to say, he can't quite place her. Then he gives all his attention to Carol and the business at hand. "My wife belongs to this joint. She likes that 'Lily and Corn' pitcher. Tomorrow's her birthday, and she's coming here for lunch. I wanna surprise her. I can write a check now."

Carol is tempted to take the check, but decides to follow procedure. "That won't be necessary, Mr. Buglio. We'll have the painting marked 'sold' by tomorrow, and you'll be billed when it's delivered after the show. All I need is an address to send the Purchase Contract to and a phone number."

Farber jumps in saying, "And we'll have 'Sold to Alice Buglio' put right on the card. What a nice surprise!"

Magpie thinks she might barf, hearing all this sickening sweetness directed toward Buglio. But she's too busy trying to stay in the shadows. She even spends some time intently studying
the Gallery calendar hanging on the wall.

The deal is closed with a handshake between Carol and Buglio. Buglio also shakes Farber's hand and moves toward the door. He moves closer to Magpie and extends his hand again, "Nice to meet ya." He gives her a steely stare and leaves the room.

Farber grabs his coat off the coat rack and starts for the door. "I hope you don't mind letting yourselves out. Just pull the door closed, the lock's on." He's halfway down the hall, and they hear him yell, "Oh, Mr. Buglio! Let me walk you to your car! I'm going that way, too!"

Carol turns to Magpie and says, "Did you expect to see him?"

"Not on your life," she answers sinking into a chair in the corner. "I wonder if he recognized me."

"He didn't seem to," Carol replies, moving to the chair next to Magpie's. "But isn't it a coincidence that he had to buy the painting tonight. There's something about this I don't like."

"There's a great deal about him I don't like," Magpie says, taking a deep breath. "But if he's willing to treat his wife to a ten thousand dollar painting, whose title he can't even remember, I'm willing to take his money."

Carol pats Magpie's arm. "Looks like they're closing shop for tonight, so let's get out of here. We have a warm bath in a cozy motel waiting for us."

"Sounds good to me," Magpie says, standing up and stretching. "I'm feeling a little tired. Seems I don't have my full energy back yet. And I can't wait to get out of this dress. Don't get me wrong. I like the color and the soft material. And with this length, I don't have to shave my legs. But a dress is a dress is a dress. I think Gertrude Stein said that."

"I think Mary Magpie York said it," Carol adds. "Because she doesn't like girl clothes." She smiles at Magpie and walks to the door. Pointing to the left, she says, "I think this is the way out."

Magpie moves very close to her and takes her hand. "Why don't we go out the back. I'd like to stand once more in the moonlight...with you next to me.
It makes me feel very much alive."

Carol starts to protest. "They may have locked that exit already." Then she gives in. "But we might as well have a look. How can I resist that kind of romance?"

They retrace their steps down the several dark corridors and find the open gallery leading to the backstair exit. This gallery is devoted to early Spanish artifacts, a king and queen's sarcophagus, various weapons of war from the Crusades, and several suits of armor surround the large room. The moonlight coming in from the two glass doors makes eerie shadows on the walls and marble floor.

Carol does a quick two-step and catches up to Magpie. "Did you hear that?" she asks in a hushed voice.

"I don't think it was anything," Magpie answers, keeping her quickened pace, as she heads for the door. Then she slows down and again takes Carol's hand and says, "Probably all this iron adjusting to the new warm temperature."

They reach the door and Magpie stops to gaze at the moon through the glass doors. She squeezes Carol's hand saying, "Okay on the count of three, we push the doors open. But be sure you have everything because we can't get back in. These doors lock behind us."

Carol takes a minute to look into the big tote-bag on her shoulder; then she gives Magpie an 'okay' nod. Together they push open the doors and walk out into the crisp evening air. From their platform above the stairs, they can see the full moon and surrounding stars, as well as the moon's reflection gleaming from the lake across the street from the gallery. They stand for a few minutes just looking at the moon and lake. Magpie puts her arm around Carol and lays her head on Carol's upper arm. Carol's cheek touches Magpie's hair.

Carol is first to break the silence. "I think we should go now," she says with concern in her voice.

Magpie lifts her head up, "Why? What's wrong?"

"I'm not sure," Carol tries to explain. "I'm just feeling very uncomfortable. I feel like someone's watching us."

"Too much excitement, maybe." Magpie tries to

reassure her. "Okay, let's get going. The parking lot's in the front anyway. So I can still hold your hand in the moonlight while we walk around this building."

They start down the stairs and pass four rows of columns, which are placed about every twelve stairs. They stop about half-way down, so Magpie can again look at the moon. As she looks up, Carol says nervously, "What was that?"

They both turn to look behind them. "Probably a bird," Magpie says unconvincingly.

They move further down the steps, hand in hand. "There it is again," Carol says with a shaky voice. "Did you hear that?"

Magpie doesn't look behind this time. She just starts to hurry, pulling Carol along with her. "I did hear it, and whoever or whatever it is seems to be right behind us."

They are hurrying now, down the remainder of the granite steps. Both hear the light footsteps behind them and neither takes the time to turn around. They are within five steps of the sidewalk when something big and dark seems to fall against them pushing both of them down the remainder of the stairs.

Carol hits the sidewalk on her arm. She starts screaming in fear, the contents of her purse scatter in front of her. Magpie is knocked on her side with the dark figure still next to her. Suddenly, she feels a kick to her stomach, and for five long seconds she can't pull any air into her lungs. Finally, she's gasping for oxygen, clutching her throbbing mid-section. The dark figure is a man. She can tell by the way he moves and by his mumbling.

"Keep out of other people's business," he growls under the black nylon he has on his face. "Go home!" he snarls, as he goes to kick her again. This time she's ready. Moving quickly to one side, she averts the kick, and he almost loses his balance. Angrier now, he comes at her with his gloved fist. She rolls away again and catches the punch in her left arm. The pain acts like a reflex action and pulls all her attention to the bruise. He moves in again and slaps her face with the back of his hand.

Magpie hits the sidewalk with her head, barely feeling the concrete scraping her cheek. He walks slowly over to her moaning limp body. He looks at Magpie and readies another kick. He swings back his leg... but something happens....

Carol is bending over behind him, grabbing his leg and twisting it, screaming, "You son-of-a bitch! You hurt her!"

He loses his balance and falls on his back. She's next to him before he can get up...kicking him in the groin with all the strength she can muster. "That's for Mary! You shithead!"

He writhes with pain, clutching his groin. She kicks him again; this time in the stomach area. He yelps and rolls over, mumbling profanities. Now she jumps on him, kneeing him in the back and pummeling him with her hands and fist.

"Carol! Carol! You're going to kill him!" Magpie's next to her, blood from her scraped face is visible in the moonlight.

Carol stops hitting him and looks at Magpie. "Oh baby!" she says, rushing to Magpie. "Oh honey, look how he hurt you." She wraps her arms around Magpie, practically crying, "Are you alright? We have to get you help."

As they hold each other, the attacker gets up and starts running around the building. Police sirens are heard, getting closer. In less than two minutes, a police car pulls up and two officers jump out. They ask the women what happened, and as Carol tries to explain, the two Gallery guards walk the captured man back around the building to the police car.

Against Carol's protests, Magpie refuses to have an ambulance called. She insists that Ginni will take care of her. The officers handcuff the man and make him stand in front of the police car. Magpie and Carol move closer, as the officer shines a flashlight on his face and slowly pulls off the stocking mask.

Neither of the women recognize the man, and he refuses to give his name or tell why he attacked them. The police put him in the back of the car and take statements from the two women. Magpie then signs a release stating she refused help for her injuries.

For a second time, Carol asks Magpie to let her drive to a hospital. Magpie again refuses, insisting she's okay and would rather let Ginni treat her. Carol presses down the gas pedal and goes over all the speed limits, heading directly for Ginni and Nikki's home.

CHAPTER 24

"Oh Nikki!...Oh No!...Oh God!" Nikki's sweaty body is on top of Ginni, moving in the undulating rhythm of her hips. Ginni has her arms wrapped around Nikki's waist, her arousal climbs with each movement, each kiss on the neck, touch to her breast, nibble on her ear.

Nikki rolls to Ginni's side. They're skin to skin, lips to lips, hands moving closer to mutual climax. The bed sheets are twisted under them; the blanket and quilt are piled on the floor where they fell. The temperature in the room is rising with the temperature in the bed. No world exists except the reality of their bodies' needs. They're lost in thrusting, searching, heat...until....

There's two quick knocks on the bedroom door, and Magpie barges in. "I'm sorry to just walk in like this...," she starts rapidly explaining. "But I used my own key, and I really need to see you Ginni. I don't feel very well since the attack, but I didn't want to go to the hospital, since they won't know about the surgery." She takes a breath.

During this first blitz, Nikki and Ginni quickly disengage and struggle to partially cover themselves with the tangled sheets. Magpie seems oblivious to their awkward bed ballet, as she goes on. "And Nikki, I really thought I should tell you what happened. Well, Buglio came to the gallery tonight to buy one of my paintings for his wife, who is a member of the gallery, he says, but I'm not sure, but then he leaves, and we walk out and this guy attacks us. I mean, he really let me have it, and he kept saying something like, 'stay out of other people's business'. And I thought I was on a one-way ticket to Never-Never Land. But Carol, where are you Carol? Come on in and fill in the blanks."

Carol, still standing in the doorway, looks very embarrassed as she's pulled further into the room. Nikki and Ginni sit up, sharing a sheet that only partially covers their bodies. They stare speechlessly at Magpie, who continues. "So the police came and the security guards from the gallery have this guy, and they take off the stocking on his face, and we don't know who he is, and he won't tell. So they take him to the station, and we came right here."

With this last statement, she instinctively puts her hand up to her forehead and winces in seeming pain. Then, taking a step forward, she grabs the footboard of the bed.

Carol moves toward her saying, "Mary, are you alright?"

Magpie goes down on her right knee and then falls to the floor. Her body stiffens and her arms and legs start to twitch in jerky muscular contractions.

Carol screams, "Mary!" And kneels next to her.

Ginni leaps from the bed, taking the sheet with her as a wrap. Nikki jumps off the bed on the opposite side and wraps the blanket, which is lying on the floor, awkwardly around her body, dragging it toward Magpie.

Ginni leans over the convulsing Magpie, ignoring the sheet as it falls away from her body. She checks Magpie's head and neck, making sure her airway is clear. She checks her pupils and examines the cheek abrasion and bump on her head where she hit the sidewalk.

Magpie is still jerking uncontrollably, as Ginni turns to Nikki and in a nervous but professional voice says, "Better call 911. She's unconscious and seizing, her breathing is very irregular." She looks back at Magpie and puts her hand on the unconscious woman's shoulder. "Tell them it's a grand mal seizure, and she's been in it about two minutes. I'm concerned that she's not breathing."

Nikki follows directions, calling the emergency number and reporting what Ginni told her. By the time she hangs up the phone and gets robes for Ginni and herself, they hear the fire siren go off. The paramedics are on their way.

❦

By the time Ginni, Nikki, and Carol arrive at Mercy Hospital, Magpie is out of the seizure and breathing on her own, even though she still wears the precautionary oxygen. Jeff Manheim was in the hospital doing a post-operative exam when he was paged to the Emergency Room to check Magpie.

He enters the crowded Waiting Room and looks for Ginni. Waving, he approaches with a file folder in his hands. "I'd like to say, good to see you again, but this doesn't seem to be the circumstances." He takes Ginni's hand and nods at Nikki and Carol. "I thought she was staying at your place, so she could rest and heal?" he says jokingly.

Then he opens a folder and comments while he reads, "She said something about being attacked...a few bruised ribs...no broken bones...abrasion on left cheek...and a slight concussion." He looks up at Ginni. "That's the problem. A head injury coming so close after the brain surgery...she was bound to seizure. I thought we were home free from the seizures when she didn't have any after the surgery. Now we'll have to wait and see."

"What do you mean, wait and see?" Carol asks, concern in her voice and on her face.

Jeff looks at her and tries to explain. "This may be a single seizure caused by the head injury, or it may be a bigger complication because the injury was combined with the recent surgery." He turns back to Ginni. "I've ordered dilantin. She's going to stay with us for a few days. If she doesn't have another one, we'll take away the drug and watch her. If she does have more, we're looking at epilepsy, and I'll start adjusting the meds."

He takes Ginni's hand again saying, "Nice to see you again, Ginni. One of you can go in there now. She's groggy but conscious." He leaves the waiting room.

Carol looks at Ginni and says questioningly, "Maybe you should go in and tell her what's happening. You're the doctor."

Ginni replies, "I think she'd rather see you first. I can always explain things to her tomorrow."

Carol turns quickly and hurries through the door.

Nikki and Ginni sit next to each other again. New patients are walking or being wheeled into the Emergency Room area in a continuous stream. A television blares and old movie, and a noticeably drunken teenage couple pound on an empty soda machine, trying to make it work.

Ginni takes Nikki's hand and in a soft voice says, "That was scary."

"I thought these medical emergencies didn't bother you doctors," Nikki says factiously.

"Except when they're friends and family." She squeezes Nikki's hand, and they smile at each other.

"Is that a good sign or a bad sign?" A rumpled, sleepy-looking Max asks, pointing to the hand-holding.

"What are you doing here?" Nikki asks, quickly letting go of Ginni's hand.

"Think I can get some coffee? Meyers woke me out of a sound sleep." He walks over to a coffee machine, fishes in his pockets for change, feeds the machine, and gingerly carries the coffee back to where Nikki and Ginni sit.

He plops in the chair next to Nikki. "Meyers called to tell me they just arrested Benjamin Conti...seems he attacked two women at the art gallery." He takes a sip of coffee before continuing. "When he told me one of them was Mary York, I tried to get hold of you. No answer, so I called Ginni's service. Good thing someone always knows where the doctor is. So how is she? The patrol cops thought she was pretty hurt."

"He beat her up good," Nikki says angrily. "She hit her head and went into a seizure. They're going to keep her here for awhile."

Max sips more coffee, then asks, "So how does this all tie in with the Fairburn and Coleman murders? Any ideas, Nikki?"

"The only connection I can think of is drugs," Nikki says, thinking as she talks. "Celine and Coleman are connected by drugs. So is Conti."

"And why was Mary attacked?" Max asks pointedly.

Nikki thinks for a minute before answering, "Maybe for the same reason I was. Somehow they found out we were involved in the case and don't want us nosing around."

Max takes several sips before commenting. "It's possible someone told Coleman you were trying to find out who murdered Celine, and that meant nosing into all her drug contacts. But who knew about Mary? And for that matter, why was Mary sniffing around in this case? You seem to have omitted that she was still involved. I thought her energy was going into getting well."

Nikki tries to explain. "She really isn't involved. I mean, she was at the Sin Club the night we went for Trang, but...well...it seems important to her to try and help figure out some of the details of Celine's murder. It seems to give her something interesting and worthwhile in her life."

"Oh, so painting and having big gallery shows isn't enough," Max says mockingly.

"All that wasn't enough," Nikki says, frustrated by his lack of understanding. "She wants to feel needed and be able to help someone."

"And so this other amateur detective named, Mary, who just wanted to help...," Max goes on. "What was she investigating without letting me know?"

"All she did, I swear, Max..." Nikki says, trying to sound repentant. "...was call an old friend of her Aunt's and try to find out where Celine's drugs might have come from."

"Oh, that's all," Max echoes back to Nikki. "And just who is this old friend, who has information like who's selling drugs?"

"His name is Uncle Lucky," Nikki hesitates, then decides to tell him everything. "Her Aunt was close friends of Luciano Spatucci."

Max suddenly chokes on a swallow, coughing and spraying the room with coffee and saliva. "Luciano Spatucci! Do you realize he's the biggest mob boss in Canada? This is her Uncle Lucky?"

Nikki tries to calm him down. "Mary says he's just a sick old man now. Like you said, just an old friend of the family."

"He may be old and sick, but he still carries a lot of power in mob circles." Max pauses to brush the sprayed coffee off his suit jacket. He turns back to Nikki and asks, "So, what did she find out from Spatucci and when did you plan to tell me?"

"She hasn't heard anything yet," Nikki says defensively. "He said he'd call when he found out something, but he hasn't yet."

"And do you think her goin' to Spatucci has anything to do with Conti and the attack?" Max asks.

"I'm not sure." Nikki rubs her forehead, trying to put the pieces together. "Before she passed out, Magpie said Buglio came to the gallery and bought one of her paintings. But that might be a coincidence."

"I don't think anything's a coincidence." Max says. "He was probably checking her out. But the Buffalo cops are

pretty sure Conti was working alone. They think he was trying
to rob the two women, that he needed cash."

"Do you think they're right?" Nikki asks.

"Can't tell," Max says, crushing the empty Styrofoam
cup. "But I think I'll be able to tell after they question him
tomorrow."

"I've got a few questions I'd like to ask him myself,"
Nikki blurts out.

Max gives her a long look and says, "Well, if you're
not too busy solving these cases yourself, why not come with
me to the interrogation. You can always slip me notes. Meyer
said I could ask some questions if he misses anything."

Nikki is so appreciative, without thinking she gets up,
wraps her arms around his neck and kisses him on the
cheek."

"Hey! Hey! Don't think that'll get you off the hook,"
he says, embarrassed by the show of affection. "You be
careful. This case is too complex to underestimate anything
or anyone...which reminds me. There is one other link
between all the people. Someone we have to look at as a
serious suspect."

"Who's that?" Nikki asks. Curiosity obvious in her
voice.

Max is very serious when he says, "Trang. She's
connected to everyone involved. Even knew Mary from the
Fort Erie adventure, and I bet you told her Mary was finding
out about the drugs, right?"

Nikki nods hesitantly. "I did mention it to her. I'm
trying to keep her posted on the case. But I'm sure she's not
behind all of this. She couldn't be, Max."

"Trang could very much be behind this," Max
punctuates each word. "I told you before, she's not the young
war victim you knew in NAM." He gets up from his chair.
"Be careful. And I moved the time up for tomorrow. I'll pick
you up at seven-thirty."

Ginni gives Max a wave as he leaves the Emergency
Room. Then she leans over and takes Nikki's arm. "He's only

looking out for you," she says softly. "He's your friend...and I trust his chubby cop instincts."

Nikki smiles at the humorous reference to Max's weight. "I know. He's going out of his way to include me in more of the police work on this case than I deserve, like tomorrow's interrogation. I can always count on Max, but...." She turns and looks Ginni in the eyes. "I don't think Trang did these things. I just can't believe that."

Ginni smiles. "Then trust your instincts. They've been pretty good before, and I think you're a beautiful and intelligent woman." She leans in further and gives Nikki a quick kiss.

✻

Carol returns to the Emergency Room and informs Ginni and Nikki that Magpie is being transferred to a room on the fourth floor. "She's pretty groggy," Carol explains. "But she knows you're here for her...and she's glad I'm here. She kissed my hand and told me to get a good night's rest." Her voice catches, and she stops for a moment before saying, "I really love that Magpie."

They all take the elevator to the fourth floor and wait for the nurse to give them the okay to go in and say good night. First Ginni approaches the bed. Magpie touches her face, and Ginni kisses the palm of Magpie's hand. "Get some rest, Mary. You're going to be fine. Jeff will see you in the morning, and I'll stop after hours tomorrow afternoon. Goodnight."

She moves away from the bed, and Carol moves in close to Magpie. She brushes back some hair off Magpie's forehead and kisses her. "I'll be back first thing in the morning. Try to sleep, and remember...I love you." She kisses her again and moves out into the hall.

Nikki walks over to the bed and makes the sign of the cross in a blessing on Magpie's forehead. Magpie motions Nikki to come down closer to her face. "Hey Leftenant, who do you think did this?"

Nikki doesn't know how much Magpie will remember in the morning but offers the explanation anyway. "It was Benjamin Conti, the guy who was selling drugs to Celine. Max just stopped by and invited me to Conti's interrogation tomorrow morning. I'll let you know what I find out." She leans over Magpie, and not wanting to hurt the cheek abrasion, kisses her gently on the lips.

"Hey Leftenant," Magpie says smiling. "I think that's the first time you ever kissed me. Now I know why all those women are chasing you," she lets out a soft laugh and coughs.

Nikki laughs with her and leans over once more. This time she puts her mouth close to Magpie's ear and says, "I love you too, Magpie. Get some rest and get well. I still need you on this case."

Magpie smiles and finally closes her eyes. The medicine she's been fighting wins the battle, and she falls asleep.

Carol, Ginni and Nikki make their way down the hall to the elevator. As the door opens and they're about to enter...Barrett stomps off.

"What's going on?" She directs the question to Nikki. "I was just having a couple of beers at the College Club Bar, and Henry Zimmer comes in. He's a paramedic with the Sheridan Fire Department, and he told me Mary was taken to the hospital. Downstairs they told me she's on this floor. What happened?"

Before Nikki can answer, Ginni interrupts and says to Nikki, "Carol is leaving her car here and coming home with us tonight. We'll wait in the car for you." They get on the open elevator and leave.

Nikki moves Barrett to the side of the hall and tries to explain the attack on Magpie. Barrett, who is a little drunk keeps moving closer to Nikki, who keeps backing away while saying, "She's asleep now, Barrett. I think it's best if you come back in the morning to see her."

"Okay," Barrett says meekly. "But I wanted to talk to you too. I need to tell you something."

Sensing much of what is to come will be influenced by what she's been drinking, Nikki asks, "What is it, Barrett?"

"My parents are getting a divorce!" she blurts out, sounding like a ten-year-old. "I'm going to be left all alone. My mother's going to Vietnam in a few days, and my father's going back to some clinic." She looks at Nikki. "I don't want to be alone."

The pain in Barrett's voice causes Nikki to touch her arm and say, "You won't be alone. I'll be here for you...." Thinking quickly she adds the disclaimer, "And Ginni is here too. You can always call, and we can all get together."

Barrett seems satisfied with the offer, even if Ginni is included. She spontaneously lunges forward and throws her arms around Nikki. Then she plants a big kiss on her lips."

"Barrett!" Nikki says wriggling out of the arm-hold. "I have to go home now, and so do you." She pushes the button for the elevator, and they ride down together.

Nikki walks Barrett to the cab she had wait for her and watches while it pulls away. Then she joins Ginni and Carol, and they head for home.

CHAPTER 25

Benjamin Conti looks tired and worried. He slouches in the uncomfortable wooden straight-back chair in the Interrogation Room. He still wears the black turtleneck jersey and black pants from the attack the night before. His daily gym work-outs are apparent in the well-sculpted muscles of his shoulders, chest, and arms.

He sneers at Max and Captain Meyers as they enter the room, then focuses on Nikki, letting his small, glassy, black eyes travel from her face down her torso. His disinterested demeanor is somewhat betrayed by the nervous blinking of his right eye and anxious twitching of his upper lip.

Max sits across the well-initialed, wooden table from him. Meyers stands next to Max, and Nikki pulls a chair behind Max, almost out of sight of Conti. "Where's my lawyer?" Conti growls to the captive audience. "I'm not saying anything until he gets here."

He eyeballs Max and says, "And what's this a cop convention or what!"

Nonplussed by the prisoner's posturing, Meyers moves his six-foot-one-inch, one hundred and eighty pounds around the table to within a foot of Conti's chair. He takes a nail file out of his jacket breast pocket and starts cleaning his nails. "Anything you want to say before your lawyer gets here," He asks, concentrating on his nails. "You know everything is being tape recorded," he adds not changing his tone or concentration.

Conti sits up a little, "I'm not saying anything! You think I'm crazy or something! Now where's my lawyer?"

There's a knock on the door and Captain Meyers walks slowly across the room, putting his file back in his pocket. He opens the door and a small man, about five-foot-two-inches tall with fine-chiseled features walks in. Almost fitting under Meyer's arm, the man ducks as Meyers pulls his hand away from the doorknob.

"I'm Nathan Grimaldi," the one hundred pound, fortyish man says, handing Meyers a business card. "I'll be representing Mr. Conti." He carries his briefcase over to where Conti sits and places it on the table next to him. He then gets an empty chair from the side wall and drags it laboriously up to the table next to Conti.

Before he sits down, he extends a hand across the table to Max. "I'm Nathan Grimaldi from Tempesto, Algieri, Rocco, and Associates."

Max stands and leans as far as he can over the table in order to reach the little man's hand. "I'm Sergeant Max Mullen. That's Nikki Barnes," he says, pointing his free hand to where Nikki sits. He deliberately omits any titles or explanations of who he and Nikki are, hoping Grimaldi just assumes they're with the department.

Grimaldi sits on the edge of his chair and opens his briefcase. He meticulously takes out a yellow legal pad and two pens. He leans over to Conti and whispers something in his ear. Conti nods and pulls away with a bothered expression. Grimaldi picks up one of the pens, turns to Meyers and says, "You may begin now."

Meyers throws a look at Max and moves closer to the table. He leans over, eye to eye with Conti and snarls,

"Why'd you attack those two women last night?"

Grimaldi leans over forcing Meyer's eye contact to move to him and says, "We haven't established that my client did attack those women?"

Meyers gives him a cold look, saying, " Both women identified him at the scene of the crime. Two security guards caught him running away, and he signed a confession less than an hour after the crime."

Grimaldi returns sheepishly to his yellow pad jotting down notes while he explains, "My client was under the influence of a narcotic substance. He is presently being treated for substance abuse and has no recall of his actions last night."

Max slams his hands on the table, causing Grimaldi to jump in his seat. "You mean he admits he attacked them but can't remember why! Is that what you want us to believe?"

"That is correct," Grimaldi whines back in his annoying nasal voice. "He can't possibly tell you what he doesn't remember."

"And could there be a way to maybe help him remember why he attacked them?" Meyers asks, walking behind Conti and Grimaldi.

"A deal might help," Conti says, sitting up and turning to face Meyers. "Let's talk a deal and maybe things'll come back to me."

"Benjamin!" Grimaldi grabs Conti by the arm and pulls him in close for a private conference.

Conti jerks his arm away and loudly puts Grimaldi in place. "You keep your wimpy hands off me! I'm not spending ten years in prison for hitting some ditzy artist!" He turns to Meyers "So do we deal or not?"

Meyers doesn't speak or look at him. He just walks slowly around the table until he's next to Max. Then he says to Conti, "I think we can possibly get the charges reduced, maybe get some of them dropped. Right Max?"

He gives Max a friendly slap on the shoulder, and Max nods in agreement.

"Of course," Meyers goes on, "You'll have to give us something worthwhile...something worth ten years away from the lifestyle you're accustomed to...away from the Big C. There ain't no snow where you'll be going."

Grimaldi whirls around to Conti, grabbing his arm again. "Keep your mouth shut, if you know what's good for you. Why do you think they sent me here. Now shut up and let me talk." He turns to Meyers, changing his tone to less aggressive. "I don't think we need a deal. My client will claim impaired judgment due to substance abuse. We can get the sentence reduced without any deal."

"Impaired judgment...hmm?" Meyers looks at Max. "How many years did that last kid pull for his impaired judgment? You remember?"

"Max shakes his head, saying, "Yeah. I think the lawyer's right. That last kid only got twelve years. Yeah, the judge gave him twelve years to correct his impaired judgment."

Conti leaps to his feet. His eye and lips twitch uncontrollably in unison. "I'm not rotting in no jail for twelve years! I'll deal! What do you want to know?"

Grimaldi is also instantly on his feet and next to Conti. In a loud whisper, he says, "Are you crazy. You say anything and your life's worth shit. Let me handle this."

Max turns around and gives Nikki a knowing glance. She nods affirmative back to him.

Conti thinks for a minute, frozen in his spot, his ticks twitching overtime. Finally, he gives the little lawyer a shove, sending him toppling over his chair and spilling his briefcase and all it holds on the floor.

"Are you crazy!" Grimaldi screams at him, trying to untangle himself and get up. "Do you want to get us both killed! You make a deal, and I'm out of here," he warns Conti.

"I want a deal, and I want it in writing," Conti says to Meyers.

Meyers knocks on the two-way mirror on the wall behind Nikki. "Get a copy of the deal and bring it in, Jerry." Meyers says to the mirrored window.

Grimaldi is back on his feet, packing his yellow pad and pens in his briefcase. "You really are nuts. I don't want any part of this," he says nervously, walking toward the door. "You're on your own now." He pounds on the door. When it opens, he's gone.

Conti plunks back down in his seat, trying to cover his nervousness with an angry grimace. There's another knock on the door and Meyers opens it, retrieving a typed copy of a deal he often uses. He puts the paper in front of Conti, who quickly reads it. "This says you'll try to get the victims to drop some charges. What if they won't," he asks angrily.

Max answers for Meyers, "They'll drop the charges, if we tell them someone else was really behind the attack."

Conti shoots him a defiant look and keeps reading. "Possible one year term. I want you to put one year, max. I want it to say, 'max'. I want out in less than a year."

"No problem," Meyers says, taking a pen from his inside pocket and writing in the word, 'max'. "Anything else you want changed," Meyers asks.

"No," Conti growls and signs the paper. Then he shoves it back to Meyers, saying, "Just sign it now, and I'll answer the questions." He looks at the empty table in front of him and mumbles to himself, "I don't owe him nothing. He never did me any favors...but I'm supposed to rot in a prison for him. Sends me a faggot lawyer, who's not worth shit. I got to do everything myself."

"There's your deal," Meyers says, pushing the paper back to Conti. "Now I'll ask you again, why did you attack those two women?"

Conti looks at the ceiling as he casually answers, "I was told to discourage the little one from butting her nose in other people's business."

"How did you know you got the right person," Meyers asks.

"I was given a picture of her from the back of some art book," Conti explains. "I was told where she'd be and for how long. I don't know where the fat bitch with her came from. That sow nearly killed me." He rubs a sore spot on his shoulder.

"Who asked you to...," Meyers pauses. "...to discourage her?"

Conti starts twitching feverishly again. Doubt is apparent in his face and his body language. "I...I'm...Not so sure...."

Meyers pushes the 'deal' paper closer to Conti's hand. The touch of the paper gives him courage, and he says, "Joe Buglio gave me the orders. I was in to him for some money. He was gonna hold back on my supply. Said it was an easy job, and then we'd be square. I think it might have been a set-up."

He looks at Meyers, trying to explain this latest insight. "I think he knew I was gonna get caught. You can't trust Joe Buglio. No one can."

Meyers walks behind Conti, going around the table a second time. Max takes over the questioning. "Why did he want her beat up?"

"I don't know!" Conti exclaims, sliding back down in his seat. "She must have been nosing in his business. That's how he takes care of people who get in his way."

"What business was she nosing into?" Max persists.

"How the hell do I know!" Conti snaps back. "He gave me the picture, told me to wait at the art gallery till he left, and then get the girl. That's what I did."

Max realizes the futility of pursuing this line of questioning anymore, so he tries to fill in some more information. "You were a friend of Kimberly Remington and the late Celine Fairburn, right?"

"I'm not sure friend is the right word," Conti says smugly, "I had business dealings with both of them."

"What kind of business?" Meyers jumps in.

Conti gives a dirty little laugh and says, "Sex and drugs business. They gave me sex, and I gave them drugs."

Nikki stands and looks at Conti as she asks, "Did you give Celine her cocaine the night she died?"

"How the hell should I know!" he yells back. "If she gave me money or a good lay, I gave her coke."

Meyers leans over the table again, nose to nose with Conti. "I'm afraid that deal," he says, tapping on the paper. "Is only for the attack on the two women. That deal doesn't work for the murder of Celine Fairburn."

"What are you talking about?" Conti is on his feet again, backing away from Meyers. "I didn't kill nobody! Don't try to frame me for that one! I gave Kim good shit that night. I snorted a few lines myself with Kim. There was nothing wrong with the coke."

"Where'd you get the coke?" Nikki asks. There's a darkness in her voice she hardly recognizes. "Who'd you get the cocaine from?"

Conti nervously looks at the three faces waiting for an answer. "I...I got it...from Buglio. I got all my coke from Buglio. But I told you the stuff was okay that night. I snorted two lines myself." He sits back down fondling the paper in front of him.

"Anything else you want to tell us, Mr. Conti," Meyers asks.

Conti shakes his head and mumbles a quiet, "no."

"Any other questions?" Meyers asks Max and Nikki.

They both also nod in the negative, and Meyers goes to the mirrored window again. "You can come and get him now, Jerry," he says to the officer behind the two-way glass.

Then he walks over to Conti and takes the paper out of his hands. "This will be right in your folder. Do you want to call another attorney or should I get a public defender?"

"I don't need nobody," Conti says, barely audible now.

"Think about it and let me know," Meyers says, leading Conti toward the door.

❧

After Conti is escorted out of the room, Meyers and Nikki join Max at the table "So, what do you think?" Meyers asks Max.

"I think he's scum," Max says, letting the words hiss through his teeth. "Capable of beating up women, selling drugs for sex, and ratting on his boss, but I don't think he killed Celine or Coleman."

Meyers nods in agreement. So Nikki asks earnestly, "If he didn't kill her, you need to go see Kimberly Remington."

"She should have some answers," Max says, getting up.

"I'm still confused over why Coleman was killed," Meyers says, as he gets up. "The way I figure, Buglio hired Coleman the way he hired Conti to convince Nikki here to stop poking around the Fairburn murder. And like Conti, Coleman got carried away with his work and almost killed you." He scratches his gray, brush-cut. "But why would Buglio, or for that matter Remington, want to kill Coleman after he did his job?"

Nikki stands, ready to leave the room with them. "The only way to find the answer to that question is like I just said, ask Kimberly Remington." She taps Max on the arm. "Do you think I could come along for that interview? I promise, I won't get in the way."

"Sure, c'mon Nikki," Meyers says, answering for Max and leading her through the door. "There's only going to be the three of us there. I don't want to spook her, and I don't have a warrant yet."

They walk together down the hall to the exit doors, then out to the parking lot.

CHAPTER 26

Meyers pulls his unmarked car into the alley next to the Bon Ami dress shop. Every parking spot on the street is taken and there's a car ahead of his in the alley. The plan is to try and get Remington to go down to the station to answer questions. If she refuses, Meyers will ask her to step into the car for questioning. Max goes with Meyers to the front entrance, while Nikki waits in the back seat of the car.

The store is bustling with at least a dozen customers when Meyers and Max enter. The cashier gives them a curt, "May I help you?"

Meyers opens his badge and shows her his identification, saying, "We need to talk to Kimberly Remington."

Max scans the room looking for her. The cashier points to the far left corner of the shop. "She's in scarves," the woman says.

Max sees her, and he points too. "There she is," he says quietly to Meyers, who starts following him through the tight departments and crowded pathways.

They get two-thirds of the way across the shop, and Remington notices them. She hastily hands a scarf to the customer she's talking to. Looking up again at the two policemen heading in her direction, she turns and walks quickly through an arch-shaped doorway by the fitting rooms. She's suddenly out of sight with Max and Meyers earnestly but gently moving people out of their way, as they try to reach the archway.

Nikki sits in the car trying to meditate. She knows that clearing her mind for a few minutes will help her see things more efficiently and more clearly. She leans her head back against the seat and closes her eyes, trying to gain relaxation. Neither her mind nor her body will rest, so she sits upright and opens her eyes. As she does, she sees Kimberly Remington dart out the side door and start running down the alley, toward the sidewalk. Right to where Meyer's car is parked.

Nikki gets out of the car and in a loud voice says, "Where are you going in such a hurry?"

Remington is jolted by the unexpected appearance of Nikki. She stops abruptly, turns, and starts running down the alley in the opposite direction. Nikki is in pursuit.

Remington reaches the end of the alley, squeezes through a row of bushes, and keeps running. She's running parallel to Edward Street, cutting across private parking areas for various business offices, heading for the parking lot and small back lawn of St. John's Episcopal Church.

Nikki isn't far behind. As she pushes through the scratchy bushes, she hears Max's voice following her. He yells, "There's Nikki! She must be chasing her!" The men enter the race, following Nikki.

Remington runs across the church parking lot, holding up her long dark-green dress so she can get longer strides. Nikki is only about five feet behind her, wondering how Remington can run so fast in the clunky construction boots she's wearing. They're both on the lawn now with Nikki gaining on Remington. Max and Meyers can be heard running across the pebbled driveway behind them.

Nikki is nearly out of breath. The muscles in her legs twinge with pain from this sudden overuse. Every summer, she spends three weeks in residence at St. John's Church, replacing the vacationing pastor, an old friend from her seminary days. That's why she's hopeful of catching up with Remington. She knows that at the very end of the church lawn there is a rather steep berm that is bound to slow Remington down.

Remington reaches the hill and underestimates the incline. Her foot slips, and she loses her balance. Clawing at the grass, she recovers her footing, but not soon enough.

Nikki takes a proverbial flying leap, arms outstretched in front of her, legs extended for distance. She lands on Remington's back, roughly pushing the woman to the ground.

"Get off me!" Remington starts screaming. "I can't breathe; you're crushing me!"

Nikki rolls off the woman but keeps a firm grip on Remington's arm. The women sit side by side, panting and huffing. Max and Meyers finally catch up. Max collapses on the other side of Remington, trying to fill his lungs with air.

Meyers stands above them, hands on his hips, talking through gasps of air. "We...need to...ask you...some questions..." He closes his mouth and licks his lips, trying to restore some moisture to them. "We can talk here...or at the station...which will it be?"

"Alright! Alright!" Remington snaps, pulling her arm away from Nikki. "What do you want now?"

"Why'd you run away?" Max asks, looking askance at her. "Why'd you take off like that?"

Remington wraps her arms around her small waist, calming down her breathing. "Because I knew you arrested Benny, and I thought maybe he told you something about me...something that wasn't true."

"He told us you were responsible for giving Celine the coke that killed her," Meyers booms down at her.

"That's a lie!" Remington shoots back. She tries to stand up, but Max holds her down on one side and Nikki on the other. "I didn't kill her," she whines, sitting back down.

Meyers crouches down, so his face is next to hers. "He told us all about Buglio," Meyers says in a more confidential tone. "And he said you must have given the bad stuff to Celine, because his stuff was okay." Meyers moves closer, so she feels his breath on her face. "He said you took care of Coleman too."

Nikki throws Max another look. They realize Meyers is lying, trying to draw out some information. They're just not sure if she'll believe him.

"I didn't kill anyone!" she defiantly screams back in his face. "Benny's a little snake. I should have known he'd say anything to save his own skin." She leans back on her hands and takes a few deep breaths, trying to compose herself.

Meyers stands again, takes out his nail file and starts to clean his nails again. Nikki gets up, stands next to him and crosses her arms. Max follows, taking a little more time to shift his weight so he can stand up. He steps next to Nikki and puts his hands in his pockets. All three stare at Remington, still sitting on the ground.

She looks up at the three and says, "Benny's information is about as good as his dick. He can never seem to get it up when you really need it."

Meyers puts his file in his pocket again and says to her, "Then why don't you give us the right information?"

"And what's in this for me," she says, jumping to her feet in one quick move. "What do I get for talking to you?"

"I can always make a deal," Meyers tells her, linking his fingers together. "But remember, if you don't talk now, I book you for murder. Someone might call your father or a few newspapers and television stations and before Buglio's lawyer can even think of getting you off—all your family and friends will know."

"I told you, I don't want my father to know any of this!" she whines at Nikki.

"I'll tell you everything I know, but you have to promise me my name stays out of this."

"I can only promise, that none of us are going to tell who we got this information from," Meyers says. "Unless you're in so deep, I have to arrest you anyway."

"I'm not involved!" she pouts and stomps her foot. "All I wanted was some good powder. That asshole, Benny, got me stuck on the stuff. And, like, it's okay, all I gotta do is put out for him. No big deal. Then a couple a weeks later, I gotta put out for this sweaty fat dude. Okay. At least he can get it up."

She starts pacing back and forth in front of Nikki, Meyers, and Max. "Then the fat guy, he turns out to be Buglio. He gets bored real easy. So, he wants someone else, something different." She looks up at Meyers, shrugs her shoulders and says, "I didn't want to lose my source, you know. So Celine really likes the coke too. I talk her into doing it just once with him. He really likes her exotic looks—and they hit it off. She even goes and lives with him, dances in his club. And he always saw to it that Benny took care of me."

Nikki tries not to show her disgust, as she asks, "What happened the night Celine got killed?"

"Okay!" Remington shoots back again. "I'm getting to that!" She paces again, staring at the grass as she explains, "Celine called me from some motel in Fort Erie. She says she's leaving her old man, Buglio, for good. She wants a little snow, cause she didn't have any to take with her. I go to Benny...and he must have called Buglio. He gives me two packets. Me and him do a couple a lines from the one. So, then I drive over and meet her in a MacDonalds. This was early, she was on a break, like ten o'clock. I don't stay, because I don't want any trouble. I leave her stash, and I split."

Max is losing all patience with this one. "So who killed her?" he asks.

"It was Buglio! Why the hell aren't you listening!" She pulls her hair for dramatic effect and goes on. "He called me, later that night, and said he took care of Celine. He said there was another packet for me if I told him where he could find her real father. I tried to tell him I didn't think Coleman was her father, but he believed Celine, I guess. So I told him where the club was in Sheridan, and he went to see him, I guess. I mean, Coleman was really hungry for drugs. Celine gave him plenty, but she was in no condition...I mean...he would do anything for a fix or a blast." Her voice trails off.

Nikki turns to Meyers and whispers, "Can't you arrest her for anything. Can't you lock her up?"

Meyers answers under his breath, "No. The lawyers'll have her out in an hour. We just have to depend on her lifestyle taking care of her." He takes Nikki's hand and puts her arm through his. Then he nods at Max, and says, "C'mon, let's get going."

The three of them turn and head back to the car. Remington is left standing on the berm, pulling her hair and pouting.

❦

Once in the car, Meyers explains the next step. "I'll have to contact Fort Erie Police and work out an arrest and extradition of Buglio. That won't be easy because of his lawyers and the mob lawyers."

"Will they still support him," Max asks. "I mean, they weren't too happy about his last arrest."

"They won't like it," Meyers says. "But they have a code to take care of their own. I think the extradition will be difficult...and winning when it goes to trial, will even be harder. Remember, he didn't really hand her the stuff. He made sure it went through two other people before it was given to her. Conti had to know which packet was for Celine, maybe Remington was in on it too. No way to get the real truth."

"You mean, Buglio may walk again?" Nikki asks, her voice betraying how upset she really is. "He kills two people, messes up God knows how many more, and we can't even get him locked up. Where's the justice?"

Max turns to Nikki and tries to reassure her. "We do our best. Maybe get the truth out of 'em, but the DA has to make the charges stick." He says in a softer voice, "At least now we know what happened, and who did the murders. And now you're safe and Mary too. Once the police contact Buglio, he'll know we have the story."

He turns back, staring out the front car window. "We'll get Conti locked up for awhile anyway...Remington will keep changing her story for whoever offers her the best deal. I guess we have to be happy with what we get."

✄

Nikki rushes through the Buffalo International Airport, hunting for the American Airlines counter. She finds the right area and joins a small group of passengers huddled around the television screen checking arrivals and departures. She's angry with herself for waiting so long to make the decision to tell Trang what she learned the day before.

Trang's plane to New York City, where she'll connect to the overseas flight to Vietnam, leaves in twenty minutes from Boarding Area Fourteen. Nikki turns around and starts running down the long corridors. She passes the consecutive numbers until she reaches Area Fourteen.

She's too late. All the passengers have passed through the security check with their luggage, and they won't let her through without a plane ticket. She can see Trang through the windows that separate the boarding area from the outside corridor. But Trang is intently marking off items on a computer print-out on her lap. The work has her full attention.

Nikki's knocks on the glass are too soft to get anyone's attention.

Frustrated, she leans against the window with her forearms. A familiar voice behind her says, "You'll never get her attention when she's working."

Nikki spins around and sees Barrett, holding a Styrofoam cup of coffee in her hand. Barrett gives her a sad smile. "I just stay here to watch her until the plane leaves. I don't even know when she's coming back." She steps closer to Nikki, and they both look through the glass at Trang. "She didn't want my father to come this time. I usually wait with him."

Nikki's touched by Barrett's sincerity, which compels her to try again to get Trang's attention. She starts feverishly slapping the thick glass. Again, there's no response from anyone in the boarding area. She dejectedly turns to Barrett and says, "I really wanted to talk to your mother before she left."

Barrett, who is several inches taller than Nikki, looks down at her and calmly says, "Well you won't get her attention that way." Reaching into her jeans pocket, she takes out a small silver whistle. The kind used to scare off attackers. Then she blows it as hard and as long as she can, causing Nikki and everyone in the corridor to cover their ears.

The shrill sound does get the attention of the boarding passengers, and Trang looks up. Seeing Nikki, she leaves her luggage and walks back through the security check and out to the corridor.

"Nikki? What are you doing here?" she says moving closer.

"I...I want to tell you what we found out," Nikki hesitates. "We know who killed Celine." Nikki pauses for a minute, phrasing her sentences in her mind first. "It was Joe Buglio. He found out she was going to leave the club and him. I guess he felt if he couldn't have her, no one could. Then Buglio told Coleman to convince me to stop

investigating. When Coleman finished the job, Buglio killed
him too. Because of his drug problem, Coleman wouldn't be
a reliable employee. If the price was right, he might tell
people about Buglio."

Nikki runs out of energy and stops talking. She
realizes, as she stands with Celine's mother and sister, how
emotional a time this has been for all of them. Barrett steps
up behind Nikki and puts an arm around her. "It's okay,
Nikki. We heard about Buglio last night. We've had time to
deal with this."

Nikki gets control back and wriggles out of Barrett's
arm. She takes a step closer to Trang and asks, "How did you
find out last night? Did Max or Meyers call you?"

Trang looks at the floor as she answers, "No, the
police haven't contacted us yet." She looks back up into
Nikki's eyes and says, "Kimberly Remington called with
information she was willing to give me for a price...I paid her
five thousand dollars to find out who really killed Celine. And
it turned out to be whom I thought...all along."

Nikki feels embarrassed. "I didn't know if I should
tell you, yesterday. I was afraid you might do something...get
another gun...try to kill him...I don't know." She tries to
justify not telling Trang immediately. "By this morning, I
knew I had to let you know...I'm sorry."

"Don't be sorry," Trang says, moving closer and
kissing Nikki on the cheek. "You did what you thought was
right." She gives Nikki a small smile. "And I don't need
another gun. I took the 9MM out of your glove compartment
the day we talked to Kimberly Remington. I slipped it in my
belt, under my jacket, when you went back to the table for my
purse."

A seriousness mixed with pain comes over Trang's
face. "Thank you, Nikki. For everything you've done for me,
in the past and recently. I never told you, I couldn't, but I'm
grateful to you. I'm going to be gone a long time, so I want

you to know that from our first meeting in Vietnam, so many years ago, I knew you would be a special person in my life. Goodbye." She leans in again and kisses Nikki gently on the lips.

Then she walks over to Barrett, and her tall daughter leans down for a hug and kiss. Trang touches Barrett's face and says, "Remember, you can always go to Nikki for help...always."

Trang walks back through the security check and picks up her luggage. The passengers are already boarding. She doesn't turn around but goes through the door to the plane.

Nikki and Barrett stare in silence at the empty waiting room.

CHAPTER 27

"I haven't had a fit since the night I was clobbered on the head," Magpie says pensively to Ginni, who tries to hide a giggle behind her hand.

"We don't call them 'fits' anymore," Ginni tries to explain. "We haven't called them 'fits' since the nineteen-forties."

Magpie slides off the hospital bed and pads over to where Carol is sitting. She sits in the chair next to Carol's and carefully tucks her legs up and under the hospital gown. Still addressing Ginni, she says, "You Americans kill me. You always like to pretty-up things with longer words. I had a fit. I haven't had any since, and Jeff's gradually taking me off the anti-fit medicine."

"I know," Ginni now smiles. "I talked to Jeff this morning. He said one more day in here, and he's releasing you. So, your room is ready at our place, or were you going back to the motel with Carol?"

"I want to talk to you and Nikki about that," Magpie says, taking Carol's hand. "Where is Nikki, anyway?"

Ginni shakes her head in mock annoyance. "She's in the hospital parking lot. We ran into Max just as we were getting out of the car.

He had something important to tell her...what else is new? She should be up any minute now."

"Well, I'm too excited to wait," Magpie says, squirming in her chair. "I'm not coming back to your place...but you know I appreciate everything you two have done for me. And I'm not going to the motel either. Carol and I are going back to Toronto for a few weeks. I'll be driving down to keep my regular appointments with Jeff, so we can meet for lunch. But anyway, as soon as he gives me a clean bill of health, we're off to London. Carol wants to come with me. She wants to meet my folks and my old friends, and I think it's time I went back for awhile. Since I won't be going alone, I think I can do it."

She stops talking and a large tear rolls down the side of her face. Carol leans over and takes her in her arms. After a moment, Magpie sits upright again and says to Ginni, "I need to put the Falklands to rest...to get them out of my system. I think I can do that with Carol, back in London. What do you think?"

Ginni comes over and bends down in front of Magpie. She puts her hands on Magpie's thighs and says, "I think the Leftenant would understand more than I do, but I'm sure you're doing the right thing. You have so much to enjoy in life. You don't need to carry all that sadness and fear around anymore. Nikki had to purge the war from her psyche, and I think you do too. And I hear London is very pretty this time of year."

Magpie leans over, and they give each other a long bear hug.

"Mary?" Carol taps Magpie on the shoulder. "Mary, look who's at the door."

Magpie and Ginnie break their warm embrace. In the doorway, wearing a light blue Oleg Cassinni suit with matching shoes and tie is Giovanni Spatucci, holding a large bouquet of white roses. "I hope I'm not intruding, but I need to talk to you Ms. York."

The three women stare at the handsome, model-looking man with their mouths open. Magpie is the first to speak. Regaining her voice, she says "Of course, Giovanni, come in." Then she says to Carol and Ginni, "Would you two excuse us for a short while."

They leave the room. Giovanni comes closer to Magpie, handing her the flowers. She takes the bouquet and smells the flowers. "They're lovely. White roses were my Aunt's favorite flower."

"Yes, I know. Grandfather told me," Giovanni says softly. "He spoke of your Aunt...and you, often. That's why I came to see you."

Magpie looks at him and nervously asks, "What's wrong? Has something happened?"

"I'm afraid so," Giovanni goes on in the same quiet voice. "Grandfather Luciano died last week. We didn't call you because it was his desire to only have a small funeral, just the family.
He was buried next to his wife and my deceased uncles. He was quite ill when you came to visit, but he enjoyed your company. All the memories you brought back for him. He died a happy man." Giovanni unbuttons his suit jacket and sits on the edge of the bed. "Grandfather was concerned that you get the information you requested. He was an honorable man, a man of his word. I also live by my Grandfather's code." He pauses for a moment before going on. "Joe Buglio gave the girl the drugs. He also hired Coleman to beat up your friend and arranged for Coleman to get some bad drugs too. Grandfather wanted you to know that."

Giovanni stands up again and walks closer to Magpie. "When information came to me about the attack on you, I knew what Grandfather would want me to do. I found out you were in this hospital, so I brought the white roses. They're really from my Grandfather, in his memory, because I respect him. I also want you to know that you never have to worry about Joe Buglio again. He'll never hurt you or any of your friends again. He has always been an embarrassment to my Grandfather and the family. He was a man with no honor...but you don't need to worry about him anymore."

He takes Magpie's hand and gives it a small shake, saying, "I want you to remember that I honor my Grandfather and always will. If you ever need my help, you can reach me at my Grandfather's house. Bona fortuna."

Giovanni lets go of her hand, turns and leaves the room.

❦

"What do you mean, he's dead!" Nikki can't believe this turn of events. "What happened?" she asks Max.

"Nobody's sure." Max tries to explain, as he kicks the tire on Nikki's car. "But I thought I should come over and tell you."

Nikki thinks for a minute, trying to put this part of the story together. "How did they find him?"

"Sergeant Bond managed to get a warrant yesterday. He went with one of his officers to Buglio's Sin Club. Seems the whole front was filled with people, some rowdy bachelor's party. When this big guy shows Bond into Buglio's office, they find him dead. Shot in the temple, twice."

Nikki's almost afraid to ask but does anyway, "Do they know who did it?"

"They're not sure, " Max begins, stepping closer to Nikki. "But he was shot with a 9MM...which is a popular gun today." He stops for a moment, looks Nikki in the eyes and asks, "You still have that gun of Trang's?"

"No. I gave it back to her," Nikki lies easily. "Do they think she shot him?"

Max shrugs his shoulders. "She's a possible suspect, but it'll be hard to question her. Seems she left for Vietnam, for an undisclosed amount of time. What do you think, Nikki? She kill him?"

"I don't think she'd do that," Nikki says quickly, trying to believe it herself. "I think she would have told me, and she didn't."

"Friends don't always tell friends everything," Max says philosophically.

Nikki thinks about what he's really saying before she asks, "Do they have any other suspects? Isn't there anyone else who might want to kill him?"

"Oh, yeah." Max unconsciously pats his stomach as he answers. "They have a list of about eleven men and women who hated him enough to kill him. Plus, no one's ruling out the mob. I agree with Meyers that they protect their own. But they also take care of their own when they step out of line—and I think Buglio was way out of line."

Just then, a handsome dark-skinned man in a designer suit walks past Nikki and Max, and gets into a black Cadillac parked nearby. They both stare at the man, as he drives out of the parking lot.

"You know who that was?" Max remarks to Nikki. "That was Giovanni Spatucci, the old man's grandson and heir to the throne. Now what the hell do you think he's doing here?"

"Maybe Magpie can tell us," Nikki answers, walking toward the hospital entrance.

Max follows hastily behind her.

❊

Nikki, over-exuberantly barges into Magpie's room, calling, "Magpie! Magpie!" She yanks the bed curtain aside before she hears an answer. There on the small hospital bed is Carol, her blouse unbuttoned, her slacks unzipped. Lying on top of her is Magpie, scampering back into her hospital gown. "What is this Nikki, tit for tat!" Magpie says, vexed by the interruption.

Max retreats to the hallway, while Nikki remembering Magpie's visit to her bedroom plunges on. "What was Giovanni Spatucci doing here? Did he tell you anything?"

Magpie is off the bed and tying the gown behind her neck. Carol is struggling to get up, zip her pants and button her blouse. "He came to tell me Uncle Lucky died," Magpie says puzzled by the question.

"Did he say anything else?" Nikki prods Magpie for more information.

"Yes. He said Buglio gave Celine the drugs, but I shouldn't worry about him anymore. The family is taking care of him. And he brought me roses." Magpie points to the flowers, now in a vase on her dresser.

"Buglio's dead." Nikki says, calming down. "Someone killed him."

Magpie's eyebrows go up. "Well, he didn't say anyone killed Buglio, just that he couldn't hurt me anymore. Maybe he just wanted me to know he was dead," Magpie offers.

"Maybe." Nikki says weakly. Then she walks over and gives Magpie a hug and kiss on the cheek. "I'm glad you're feeling better. Sorry about my untimely entrance. I need to find Ginni, but I'll be back."

Nikki goes out to the hallway and asks Max, "Did you hear that?"

Max nods a 'yes'.

As they walk down the hall, Nikki continues her rationalization. "So maybe the mob killed him."

"Or maybe, Trang killed him," Max replies.

"We'll never know for sure, will we?" Nikki asks rhetorically.

"Not unless Trang tells you for sure, or a mobster turns state evidence, " Max says, getting ready to board the elevator. "And I think the chances of either are pretty slim."

Max gets on the elevator and holds the door open for one last request. "How about you and Ginni coming over for pasta on Sunday? Rosa and the boys would love to see you."

Nikki thinks for a minute about the possibilities of getting back to a normal routine. "That's a date, Max. Ginni and I will be there Sunday."

"Twelve sharp," Max points at his watch for emphasis.

Nikki smiles at her friend. "Twelve sharp," she echoes back to him.

RETURN TO ISIS $9.99
Jean Stewart

It is the year 2093, and Whit, a bold woman warrior from an Amazon nation, rescues Amelia from a dismal world where females are either breeders or drones. During their arduous journey back to the shining all-women's world of Artemis, they are unexpectedly drawn to each other. This engaging first book in the series has it all-romance, mystery, and adventure.
A Lambda Literary Award Finalist

ISIS RISING $11.99
Jean Stewart

In this stirring romantic fantasy, the familiar cast of lovable characters begins to rebuild the colony of Isis, burned to the ground ten years earlier by the dread Regulators. But evil forces threaten to destroy their dream. A swashbuckling futuristic adventure and an endearing love story all rolled into one.

WARRIORS OF ISIS $11.99
Jean Stewart

The third lusty tale is one of high adventure and passionate romance among the Freeland Warriors. Arinna Sojourner, the evil product of genetic engineering, vows to destroy the fledgling colony of Isis with her incredible psychic powers. Whit, Kali, and other warriors battle to save their world, in this novel bursting with life, love, heroines and villains.
A Lambda Literary Award Finalist

EMERALD CITY BLUES $11.99
Jean Stewart

When comfortable yuppie world of Chris Olson and Jennifer Hart collides with the desperate lives of Reb and Flynn, two lesbian runaways struggling to survive on the streets of Seattle, the forecast is trouble. A gritty, enormously readable novel of contemporary lesbigay life, which raises real questions about the meaning of family and community. This book is an excellent choice for young adults and the more mature reader.

ROUGH JUSTICE $10.99
Claire Youmans

When Glenn Lowry's sunken fishing boat turns up four years after is disappearance, foul play is suspected. Classy, ambitious Prosecutor Janet Schilling immediately launches a murder investigation, which produces several surprising suspects-one of them, her own former lover Catherine Adams, not living a reclusive life on an island. A real page-turner!

NO WITNESS $9.99
Nancy Sanra

This cliffhanger of a mystery set in San Francisco, introduces Detective Tally McGInnis, whose ex-lover Pamela Tresdale is arrested for the grisly murder of a wealthy Texas heiress. Tally rushes to the rescue despite friends' warnings, and is drawn once again into Pamela's web of deception and betrayal as she attempts to clear her and find the real killer.

DREAMCATCHER $9.99
Lori Byrd

This timeless story of love and friendship illuminates a year in the life of Sunny Calhoun, a college student, who falls in love with eve Phillips, a literary agent. A richly woven novel capturing the wonder and pain of love between a younger and an older woman.

DEADLY RENDEZVOUS $9.99
Diane Davidson

A string of brutal murders in the middle of the desert plunges Lt. Toni Underwood and her lover Megan into a high profile investigation, which uncovers a world of drugs, corruption and murder, as well as the dark side of the human mind. Explosive, fast-paced, & action-packed.

DEADLY GAMBLE $11.99
Diane Davidson

Las-Vegas-city of bright lights and dark secrets-is the perfect setting for this intriguing sequel to *DEADLY RENDEZVOUS*. Former police detective Toni Underwood and her partner Sally Murphy are catapulted back into the world of crime by a letter from Toni's favorite aunt. Now a prominent madam, Vera Valentine fears she is about to me murdered-a distinct possibility.

FEATHERING YOUR NEST: An Interactive Workbook& Guide to a Loving Lesbian Relationship
Gwen Leonhard, M.ED./Jennie Mast, MSW $14.99

This fresh, insightful guide and workbook for lesbian couples provides effective ways to build and nourish your relationships. Includes fun exercises & creative ways to spark romance, solve conflict, fight fair, conquer boredom, spice up your sex lives.

TROPICAL STORM $11.99
Linda Kay Silva

Another winning, action-packed adventure featuring smart and sassy heroines, an exotic jungle setting, and a plot with more twists and turns than a coiled cobra. Megan has disappeared into the Costa Rican rain forest and it's up to Delta and Connie to find her. Can they reach Meagan before it's too late? Will Storm risk everything to save the woman she loves? Fast-paced, full of wonderful characters and surprises. Not to be missed.

STORM RISING $12.00
Linda Kay Silva

The excitement continues in this wonderful continuation of *TROPICAL STORM*. Another incredible adventure through the magnificent rain forest leaves the reader breathless! The bond that connects Storm and Connie, shines through the most difficult challenges. This story gives the reader an incredible ride of adventures in the physical and spiritual dimensions.

AGENDA FOR MURDER $11.99
Joan Albarella

A compelling mystery about the legacies of love and war, set on a sleepy college campus. Though haunted by memories of her tour of duty in Vietnam, Nikki Barnes is finally putting back the pieces of her life, only to collide with murder and betrayal.

NO ESCAPE $11.99
Nancy Sanra

This edgy, past-paced whodunit set in picturesque San Francisco, will keep you guessing. Lesbian PI tally McGinnis is called into action when Dr. Rebecca Toliver is charged with the murder of her lover Melinda. Is the red rose left at the scene the crime the signature of a copycat killer, or is the infamous Marcia Cox back, and up to her old, evil tricks again?

DANGER IN HIGH PLACES $9.99
Sharon Gilligan

Set against the backdrop of Washington, D.C., this riveting mystery introduces freelance photographer and amateur sleuth, Alix Nicholson. Alix stumbles on a deadly scheme, and with the help of a lesbian congressional aide, unravels the mystery.

DANGER! CROSS CURRENTS $9.99
Sharon Gilligan

The exciting sequel to *Danger in High Places* brings freelance photographer Alix Nicholson face-to-face with an old love and a murder. When Alix's landlady turns up dead, and her much younger lover, Leah Claire, the prime suspect, Alix launches a frantic campaign to find the real killer.

HEARTSONE AND SABER $10.99
Jacqui Singleton

You can almost hear the sabers clash in this rousing tale of good and evil, of passionate love between a bold warrior queen and a beautiful healer with magical powers.

PLAYING FOR KEEPS $10.99
Stevie Rios

In this sparkling tale of love and adventure, Lindsay West an oboist, travels to Caracas, where she meets three people who change her life forever: Rob Heron a gay man, who becomes her dearest friend her lover Mercedes Luego, a lovely cellist, who takes Lindsay on a life-altering adventure down the Amazon; and the mysterious jungle-dwelling woman Arminta, who touches their souls.

LOVESPELL $9.95
Karen Williams

A deliciously erotic and humorous love story in which Kate Gallagher, a shy veterinarian, and Allegra, who has magic at her fingertips, fall in love. A masterful blend of fantasy and reality, this beautifully written story will delight your heart and imagination.

NIGHTSHADE $11.99
Karen Williams

Alex Spherris finds herself the new owner of a magical bell, which some people would kill for. She is ushered into a strange & wonderful world and meets Orielle, who melts her frozen heart. A heartwarming romance spun in the best tradition of storytelling.

HOW TO ORDER

TITLE	AUTHOR	PRICE
❑ Agenda for Murder	Joan Albarella	11.99
❑ And Love Came Calling	Beverly Shearer	11.99
❑ Called to Kill	Joan Albarella	12.00
❑ Coming Attractions	Katherine Kreuter	11.99
❑ Danger! Cross Currents	Sharon Gilligan	9.99
❑ Danger in High Places	Sharon Gilligan	9.95
❑ Deadly Gamble	Diane Davidson	11.99
❑ Deadly Rendezvous	Diane Davidson	9.99
❑ Dreamcatcher	Lori Byrd	9.99
❑ Emerald City Blues	Jean Stewart	11.99
❑ Feathering Your Nest	Leonhard/Mast	14.99
❑ Heartstone and Saber	Jaqui Singleton	10.99
❑ Isis Rising	Jean Stewart	11.99
❑ Love Spell	Karen Williams	9.95
❑ Nightshade	Karen Williams	11.99
❑ No Escape	Nancy Sanra	11.99
❑ No Witness	Nancy Sanra	11.99
❑ Playing for Keeps	Stevie Rios	10.99
❑ Return to Isis	Jean Stewart	9.99
❑ Rough Justice	Claire Youmans	10.99
❑ Shadows After Dark	Ouida Crozier	9.95
❑ Side Dish	Kim Taylor	11.99
❑ Storm Rising	Linda Kay Silva	12.00
❑ Sweet Bitter Love	Rita Schiano	10.99
❑ Tropical Storm	Linda Kay Silva	11.99
❑ Warriors of Isis	Jean Stewart	11.99
❑ You Light the Fire	Kristen Garrett	9.95

Please send me the books I have checked. I have enclosed
a check or money order (not cash], plus $4 for the first book
and $1 for each additional book to cover shipping and handling.
Or bill my Visa/Mastercard
Card #_____Exp. Date_____
Name (please print)_____Signature_____
Address_____
City _____State_____Zip_____
AZ residents, please add 7% tax to total.
RISING TIDE PRESS, 3831 N. ORACLE RD., TUCSON AZ 85705
Or visit our website, www.risingtidepress.com